T0130110

Making room

BOBBE TATREAU

iUniverse®

MAKING ROOM

Copyright © 2020 Roberta Tatreau.

All rights reserved. No part of this book may be used or reproduced by any means, graphic, electronic, or mechanical, including photocopying, recording, taping or by any information storage retrieval system without the written permission of the author except in the case of brief quotations embodied in critical articles and reviews.

iUniverse books may be ordered through booksellers or by contacting:

iUniverse
1663 Liberty Drive
Bloomington, IN 47403
www.iuniverse.com
1-800-Authors (1-800-288-4677)

Because of the dynamic nature of the Internet, any web addresses or links contained in this book may have changed since publication and may no longer be valid. The views expressed in this work are solely those of the author and do not necessarily reflect the views of the publisher, and the publisher hereby disclaims any responsibility for them.

Any people depicted in stock imagery provided by Getty Images are models, and such images are being used for illustrative purposes only.
Certain stock imagery © Getty Images.

ISBN: 978-1-5320-9339-5 (sc)
ISBN: 978-1-5320-9340-1 (e)

Print information available on the last page.

iUniverse rev. date: 01/23/2020

Chapter 1

As though she were trespassing in a stranger's house, Kara Talmadge stood in the narrow entry hall, surveying the maze of packing boxes and furniture crammed into the unfamiliar living room. The furniture was definitely hers: the brown and beige sectional, an upholstered rocker with a muted rust/brown pattern, end tables, and lamps. The walls were freshly painted with just a hint of russet, the off-white crown molding making the room look larger. The painter that her daughter-in-law hired had perfectly matched the paint chip colors that Kara picked out. In one wall, a triple sliding glass door opened onto a small patio made of some material that, supposedly, would never need to be stained. And beyond, a narrow garden strip waiting for the touch of spring.

Yesterday, it had been spring in Southern California. But driving east on I-40 for almost five hundred miles had brought her to the remnants of winter and a split-level condo half the size of her sprawling ranch-style house in Torrance. And half the price. That difference was what finally convinced her to move near her son's young family in Flagstaff. Since Michael's sudden death seventeen months ago, she could no longer afford to live in California. Their modest savings, his woefully inadequate life insurance policy, the small income she'd receive from selling Michael's share of the law practice, and the equity in their home were all that was left of thirty years together.

And two adult children.

"Mrs. Talmadge, I need your signature." The younger of the two movers handed her a clipboard.

"Of course." Using his pen, she scrawled her name on the line marked with the X. "Thank you for everything."

He tore the NCR sheets apart, giving her the yellow copy. "No trouble. Have a nice day." The movers still had a small load to deliver in Sedona.

Silence settled around her.

Now what?

Months of activity: selling the law firm to Michael's partner, Adam, selling the house she and Michael had lived in for a decade, buying this place, and saying goodbye to friends with whom she had less and less in common. Rushing around as though she were going somewhere important, accomplishing something. In reality, her only accomplishment was shrinking the borders of her existence. Piggybacking onto her son's family.

Friends cooed: *You'll get to watch the twins grow up. Be near family. You're so lucky.*

Kara did not feel lucky. She was pretty sure she would not truly be a part of her family's everyday lives because they were young and busy with jobs and play dates, while she was closing in on fifty, in a new city without a job or play dates. She'd always believed that parents who moved closer to their grown children had somehow given up on their own lives, trying to hang onto an outgrown familial closeness. Yet here she was on Jeff's doorstep. He worked long hours as the assistant to Flagstaff's city manager; Ellen worked part time in one of the local library branches and looked after the four-year old twins, Jared and Molly. For the time being, Kara would be a convenient and willing baby sitter because she didn't have anything else to fill her days. But at some point, she would have to find work. The money wouldn't last all that long.

She really needed a life of her own. Preferably filled with something she wanted to do. If only she knew what that was.

It was still daylight when she locked the front door behind her and crossed the stepping-stones to her three-year old silver Outback parked in the driveway. Ellen had invited her to dinner. Jeff was attending the weekly City Council meeting and would be home late. At least she didn't have to go in search of take out. Tomorrow she'd have to find a grocery store.

Once in her car, she set the GPS for Jeff's address east of town. Not the time to get lost. She needed to find a map of the city—a paper map, not some disembodied voice telling her to turn left in one hundred feet. She had no idea what one hundred feet looked like.

She woke to sharp sunlight. Day two in this strange new place. Like the living room, her bedroom was crowded with boxes, one of them with bedding spilling out. Last night, she'd clumsily made up the king-sized bed after standing in the shower until the water cooled. She was lying on a fitted sheet with only a deep blue comforter over her. No pillowcase on the pillow. Finding a top sheet and pillowcase had been beyond last night's energy level. Anti-climax had set in.

Her watch on the nightstand said 10:30. Nearly twelve hours since she'd crawled under the comforter. In her other life, she never slept this late. When Michael was still alive, she would already be at the law office, working on the accounts, leaving around noon to run errands or meet friends. Michael kept his own schedule, seldom getting home before six, usually bringing work with him.

This morning, no one would know or care if she went back to sleep. Not necessarily a good thing. Instead of ruminating about her situation or mentally berating Michael for having the nerve to die and leave her to reinvent her life, she shoved the comforter off. She really needed to pee.

Because there was nothing in the house for breakfast, she slipped on a pair of black yoga pants and a lightweight gray sweater, then set off to find a grocery store or fast food restaurant, whichever came first. Burger King won. A breakfast burrito and coffee at a garish orange plastic table. She couldn't finish the burrito, which was larger than she'd expected, and didn't want to finish the bitter, bottom-of-the-pot coffee. She needed to locate an upscale coffee shop.

Her move to Arizona had been Jeff's idea. "It makes sense financially. And you can spend more time with the twins. They need contact with at least one grandparent. They barely know Ellie's folks. Getting to their place in Maine is complicated, whether we drive or fly. And her parents seldom leave Maine. Just like Dad, never wanting to go anywhere."

Saving money and being near her grandchildren. At that moment, a combination hard to resist. After the twins arrived, she and Michael had flown to Flagstaff for a weekend every other month and had been making plans to take them to Disneyland on their next birthday. Fortunately no one had told the children about the trip, so there would be no need to deal with their disappointment. Kara couldn't afford such an expensive gift until she had a job.

It took an hour in the Safeway to find the items she needed to begin stocking her kitchen. Not knowing the store's layout had her searching for everything on her list in all the wrong places. There was something to be said for familiarity.

As she emptied the grocery bags onto the kitchen counter, she was confronted with how small this kitchen was: Which cupboard for spices? Canned goods? Pots and pans? Dishes? In her California house, the kitchen's center island had provided an extra surface with plenty of storage beneath. And she'd had a floor to ceiling pantry. This kitchen wouldn't handle major shopping excursions, but then she would mostly be cooking for herself— occasionally for the family. She'd just have to go to the store more often.

She had far too much kitchen stuff. Some of it would have to be stored until she had a better idea what a single woman needed. If her daughter, Lindsay, lived closer, she could give her a few things, but Lindsay was teaching in Hilo, Hawaii, sharing a small beach house with two other elementary school teachers. For them, pots and pans weren't as important as the condition of the surf. Most of Lindsay's high school years had been spent on Southern California beaches, and attending the University of Hawaii had only reinforced the beach lifestyle that her twenty-five year old daughter preferred. So different from Jeff, who had earned his MBA by the time he was Lindsay's age and was already something of a workaholic—like his father.

Maybe Lindsay would visit when her school was out in June, but Kara wasn't counting on it. Michael's death had so shaken his daughter that she'd flown back to Hawaii the morning after the memorial service in Manhattan Beach, not wanting comfort and not providing any, occasionally texting her mother but not sharing anything important. Acting as though it was somehow Kara's fault that Michael was dead.

Two days later, Ellen brought the twins over after she picked them up from pre-school. Blond like their mother, their father's gray eyes, and their very own smiles. Molly's fair hair was pulled back with Cinderella clips, a girly touch that contrasted with her sweatshirt and denim pants. Jared's fair hair was cropped short so it didn't have to be combed every morning. Combing encouraged complaint: *It hurts!* Molly laughing at him only made the complaints increase in volume.

While Kara savored the coffee Ellen had brought her from Starbuck's, the twins played educational games on their mini tablets. Kara wasn't convinced the children should already be absorbed with electronic toys, but her old-fashioned opinion would undoubtedly not be welcome. Admittedly, the games kept them quiet.

"Is there anything I can help you with before I take these two terrors home and turn them loose in the backyard?" Kara thought Ellen looked like she could use a nap. Working three mornings a week, keeping track of active pre-schoolers, and managing the household probably didn't give her much time for herself. Kara vividly remembered what that was like. Now she had too much time.

"Thanks for the offer, but I'm going to unpack a little at a time. Mostly because I haven't decided where anything should go. It's been a long time since I set up a house from scratch." Whenever she and Michael had moved, there was an excitement about exploring their new space and a new neighborhood. She missed those simple kinds of sharing. Maybe she'd just live out of boxes for a while. "I promise to find my Keurig so you don't have to bring me coffee next time."

It took ten minutes to get the twins organized and into the white minivan. Kara hugged all three of them and watched until the van was out of sight. Standing in the driveway, she surveyed her new street, a series of gray and white fourplex townhouses huddled together with narrow bands of artificial turf separating each group. Nothing resembling the large lawn surrounding her California house. Here there was no room for the twins to play outside safely. She'd have to take them to the city park bordering the complex, maybe a ten-minute walk.

This wasn't the way she had imagined her life would turn out. Not that she'd planned anything specific, but she had expected Michael to stick around longer. Living on her own was not part of the equation. She'd moved from her parents' home to the UCLA dorm, then into Michael's Westwood apartment after the wedding. Jeff was born seven months later. She dropped out of UCLA to take care of the baby and work part time at a local bookstore. As the children grew, there were other apartments. After

Michael passed the California bar and was hired by a major LA law firm, they bought their first house, only two bedrooms but with a backyard for the children. Then another, larger house and finally the one in Torrance.

Until Jeff was hired by the City of Flagstaff—he called it Flag—she had no idea where the city was because, once Michael opened the law practice, they seldom left the state. He was no good at relaxing for longer than a weekend in San Francisco or Tahoe.

Bottom line, nothing had predicted she'd be living in Arizona. By herself.

Chapter 2

Without a fixed schedule or job, Kara felt like a kite with no one holding the string—floating here, then there. Not exactly alone, not exactly belonging. So far, she was on a first name basis with the baristas at City Center Java and occasionally joined two younger women in her neighborhood for walks on weekends. Because they were in much better shape than she was, Kara had to push herself to keep up. On the plus side, she lost three pounds.

The packing boxes were gone by the end of May when the twins' preschool let out. Because Ellen worked at the East Flagstaff Public Library from 10 to 2 Monday, Wednesday and Friday, Nana was needed on those days. Kara could now drive to Jeff's without the GPS. It was easier to take care of the twins at their house—with all of their toys available. Kara's place wasn't particularly kid friendly. At their house, they had a safe cul-de-sac to ride their bikes, a swing set, and a grassy back yard where they could play with their friends. Sometimes there were three or four additional kids staying for lunch. Kara was learning what foods each of her grandchildren preferred and what TV programs they were allowed. On Fridays, Molly went to a late afternoon ballet class and Jared took tumbling. He wanted no part of dancing but wasn't quite ready for T-ball. Of necessity, two car seats had taken up residence in the Outback. Thankfully, Jeff had picked up that tab.

Since her arrival, Kara had seen very little of her son. Jeff often worked fourteen hour days and weekends. In early June, she took the family out for dinner on Ellen's birthday, and one Sunday afternoon in July, Jeff drove the family through the lush Oak Creek Canyon to Sedona, stopping for lunch at the Wildflower Bread Company. After lunch, they took the twins to Sunset Park to run off their energy before the drive home. While Ellen was making sure they weren't taking unnecessary risks on the playground's elaborate climbing frame, Kara used the opportunity to ask Jeff how she should go about finding work. "I've never had to look for a job. Never even been interviewed. A college friend got me the job at the bookstore, and your father was more than willing to have me take over Heather's job." No *c.v.* required.

Jeff was stretched out on the lawn, a rare moment of relaxation. He shaded his eyes to look at her. "Do you want to do what you were doing in Dad's office?"

"Not if I can help it. Being confined to an office cubicle is deadening. I'd like something where I have contact with people. Otherwise, I might become a strange old lady who talks to her cats—if I had cats."

He laughed. Such a nice laugh, though he didn't use it enough. Michael had that same seriousness.

They sat silently for a while, then "Have you thought about a job connected with art? I know you still sketch once in a while. There's an art store on Fourth Street. You could ask there."

"Actually, I've been wondering about the Museum."

"I think a lot of their people are volunteers. Let me ask Josie," his assistant, "for suggestions; she has friends everywhere. What happened to all your artwork? Did you bring it with you?"

"Yes. Everything's in storage boxes in the garage." She hadn't looked at her art for years; she simply told the movers to pack everything in that closet. Painting belonged to another Kara.

Once Jeff fell asleep, she took the opportunity to really look at her busy, super-smart son. Amazing that he was almost thirty-one. He still had a mop of brown hair that insisted on falling over his forehead. Not curly, but thick. He'd have hated curls. Lindsay had always envied her brother's hair. Hers was the same color, but fine and stick straight. Like his father, Jeff had a small cleft in his chin and, when they were open, soft gray eyes that made you trust him. She'd been fooled by them a few times when he was little and prone to lie about emptying the cookie jar or sloshing through puddles in his new shoes. Lindsay, on the other hand, was incapable of selling a lie. Her brown eyes—compliments of some unknown ancestor—gave her away every time.

Kara had been a stay-at-home mom until Lindsay entered middle school and Michael's bookkeeper moved to Seattle. Suddenly, Kara had a part time job; taking care of billable hours, the payroll, and office expenses was simpler than working a nine to five job somewhere else. At Michael's, she could set her own hours and, if one of the children was ill or had a special school event, she was able to take time off. So long as the work got done, Michael didn't care. He and Adam were obsessed with all things legal and willingly avoided the non-legal bits and pieces of running the office. In the beginning, a suitable arrangement for everyone. But after ten plus years, Kara had been restless, *let's face it*, bored by the sometimes mindless routine.

One year—to distract herself—she bought a gym membership but discovered that working out on machines was equally boring. A few months before Michael's death, she'd dug out her watercolors and set up the card table in Jeff's old room. But resurrecting what had been her high school and college passion wasn't easy. She completed only one mediocre painting before Michael died.

And her life hit a wall.

Ten days after Kara's conversation with Jeff, Josie Rios called Kara's cell while she was walking with her neighbors. "I have a lead on a part time opening at the Museum."

"Doing what?"

"The woman who has been managing the front desk in the lobby on weekends is moving to Las Vegas. You'll be selling tickets, checking memberships, giving out museum maps. Answering all kinds of questions. Just Saturday and Sunday."

"When would the job start?"

"Not sure."

Kara took a deep breath; not what she imagined but no cubicle was involved. Then, "Who's the contact?"

"Maddy West. I'll text you her number."

Maddy returned Kara's call on Sunday afternoon of the weekend Kara was taking care of the twins while Jeff and Ellen were attending a three-day city-governance conference in Chicago. Jeff was dutifully sitting in meetings; Ellen was enjoying the city's museums and shopping without the twins in tow. And Kara was discovering that three full days with her grandchildren was physically hard work. No need of a gym membership to get exercise. Fortunately, Jared and Molly were well-behaved, most of the time, but they were constantly moving, needing, asking. Kara had forgotten what it was like not to have a free moment.

"Kara? This is Maddy West. Sorry to delay getting back to you. I was sick for a few days. Josie said you might be a good fit for the opening at the Museum."

"She told me the same thing. Can you give me just a minute while I check on my grandchildren?" She hurried into the kitchen to look out the window over the sink. Jared, Molly and Susie, a red-headed friend from their preschool, were playing on the swings in the back yard. Susie was pushing Molly. Jared was standing on the other swing seat, experimenting with getting his legs to pump himself. She wanted to caution him to get down but curbed her helicopter grandmothering, staying near the window, just in case. "Sorry, I wanted to make sure they were okay. Their parents are out of town this weekend."

"No problem. Let me tell you about the job." Kara heard a bit of an accent, maybe Texan. "Seven hours on Saturday, five on Sunday. Selling admission tickets or checking memberships at the entrance. Giving out the information on current exhibits, answering all sorts of questions. It's a little of everything."

Pretty much what Josie had said. "I think I'd like that. I don't want to be in an office anymore."

"Good. Can you come in on Tuesday? I'll alert my boss so you two can meet."

"What time?" Not that it mattered. Ellen and Jeff would be back Monday afternoon. And she seldom took care of Jared and Molly on Tuesdays.

"Ten o'clock? Before Chet gets busy. If you get the job, you can shadow me for a day or two. See what I do."

Though she needed a job, the prospect of another new place, new people, and new things to learn was more unsettling than she'd expected. New on top of all the new she'd been coping with since Michael's death.

How long would it take for her days to be familiar—not boring—just easier to navigate. A rhetorical question with no immediate answer.

Kara had visited the Museum of Northern Arizona several times with Ellen and the twins, so she was familiar with Fort Valley Road and the Museum parking area. But today the imposing two-story entrance felt a little intimidating. Her stomach was queezy with nerves. What if this Chet Repik didn't find her suitable? She'd stressed over what to wear, not too formal, not too casual, ending up with tan chinos and a sleeveless cotton tunic. After all, it was still summer and this was Arizona.

The entry area was cool, dimly lit to make it seem cooler than the ninety degree outside temperature. A young couple with a sleeping boy in a stroller were at the counter, talking to a tall woman with richly black hair pulled back into a coil at the nape of her neck. Kara wondered if she was Native American.

When the family moved away from the counter, Kara asked, "Are you Maddy?"

"Yes," her wide smile made Kara relax. "And you're Kara." They shook hands. "Let me take you to Chet's office." Maddy led the way along a short hall, also dimly lit. "Don't be nervous. He's easy to talk to."

One of the hardest things about being on her own was not having someone to listen to the details—good and bad—of her day. Even when Michael was distracted, she at least hoped that he was listening. Sharing daily details with Ellen seemed unfair. Her daughter-in-law had enough details of her own. Kara hated to impose. Since she really needed to tell someone about her successful job interview, she checked the time difference between Arizona and Hawaii and called Lindsay.

"You're going to do what?"

Lindsay's tone did not suggest the kind of support Kara was looking for. She again explained the Museum job.

"Why?"

"Because I need the income and something to do." She tried to keep the exasperation out of her voice but didn't completely succeed. How could she have a daughter so lacking in tact? So uninterested in what her mother was doing.

"I thought you moved to Arizona so you could look after the twins."

Not only did Lindsay lack tact, she didn't listen any better than her father. All Kara had wanted was a *Good for you* from her daughter. To keep from telling Lindsay she had hurt her mother's feelings, Kara changed the subject. "When do classes begin?"

"Two weeks."

"Second grade again?"

"A second and third combined. I'm working my butt off trying to figure out how to make that happen."

"I'm sure you'll do fine. How's the surfing?"

With that, Lindsay became upbeat and garrulous. After three minutes of listening to wave heights and water temperatures, Kara tuned out, quite aware she wasn't listening any better than her daughter had listened to her.

In frustration, Kara lied about having an appointment and said goodbye. What had made her think Lindsay would be interested?

After three weekends at the Museum, Kara was settling into the job, her confidence increasing with every visitor question she was able to answer correctly. And she was doing better making change. An unexpected plus was having something that filled her weekends. She hadn't realized how often people would ask—probably because they couldn't think of anything else to say—*How was your weekend?*

The simple answer was—*Fine*—even though it wasn't fine at all. In the current culture, weekends were family times or times when couples went out to dinner or to parties. Kara, however, was on the sidelines, watching the rest of the world living the life she'd once had. Seeing couples of any age holding hands still made her tear up. Michael had always held her hand when they walked even short distances. Because the Museum was becoming her weekend, her answer changed to "I was working." And she didn't care if the person asking replied, "Oh that's too bad." She had some place to be on Saturday and Sunday. And going home tired was okay. It was a good tired.

She spent a few Tuesday afternoons touring the Museum, getting acquainted with exhibits like *The Trappings of the American West*, then browsing the gift shop to talk to the staff about Navajo rugs or jewelry—a crash course in the Colorado Plateau culture. She borrowed books from the Museum library and spent her evenings reading. Slowly she was carving out a small niche for herself. The other staff members knew her name, and sometimes they shared coffee breaks.

Along with learning her new job, Kara was adjusting to a new climate. Fall in Southern California was often hot; the Santa Ana winds terrorizing the inhabitants with fears of fire and one hundred degree heat. The temperatures might not cool down until late October, but fall in Flagstaff came closer to what the calendar and the autumnal equinox expected.

The twins began kindergarten the week before Labor Day so there was no fixed babysitting schedule for Kara while Ellen was at work. The second week of September, Jeff unexpectedly flew to Cincinnati. The day after he returned, he showed up on her doorstep just after seven o'clock.

"What a nice surprise." Delighted but puzzled by his unannounced solo appearance, she kissed his cheek. "Do you want coffee? Wine?"

"Do you have red?"

"I do." She kept it on hand especially for him.

She brought him a glass of Merlot, white for herself, and sat in the rocking chair. "How was Cincinnati?"

"Stormy, compliments of Canada." He didn't elaborate.

Sensing that he was nervous, she waited. Clearly, he had a mission.

Finally she couldn't stand the tension. "What's wrong? Is someone ill? Did someone die?"

He shook his head. "Neither of the above." An awkward pause. "I have a new job."

"I'm assuming that's good news?"

"Yes and no," he hesitated, "it's in Cincinnati."

It took her a moment to process *Cincinnati*. As in Ohio.

"You're leaving Flagstaff?" Her voice rose slightly. How could he possibly be going all the way to Ohio when she was rebuilding her life—here. To be near him. To watch her grandchildren grow up.

Rushing ahead, "You have to understand it's a huge step up." He was little-boy earnest. "Cincinnati's a much larger city, more possibilities, definitely more money and better benefits." Proudly, "They head-hunted me. Said I was a perfect fit."

"But don't you have a contract here? How can you just quit?" She knew her voice was harsh. A knot of panic was twisting her stomach.

"Actually, my current contract was up in August and, since my boss knew Cincinnati was interested in hiring me, this contract has been on hold. Everyone here has been really supportive."

"How nice of them." He probably didn't hear her sarcasm.

He'd known he would be leaving for at least a couple of months and said nothing!

She measured out her words, a sure sign of anger, "How does Ellen feel about this?"

"She's on board."

Of course she would be. Wives did that. Similar to Michael leaving the prestigious LA law firm he worked for to go out on his own. Wives were on board. What choice did they have?

"I'm sorry I didn't tell you till now, Mom. You understand, don't you?"

He looked as though he'd just owned up to raiding the cookie jar, but Kara was in no mood to forgive—or *understand*.

She forced herself to sound calm. "When does this happen?"

"The middle of October. We listed the house today. I have someone looking for a temporary rental in Cincinnati. Once this house sells, Ellie and the kids will join me and we'll look for a house to buy."

And that leaves me here.

In Arizona.

By myself.

First Michael. Now Jeff.

His duty done, he checked his watch, finished the last of his wine, and stood up. The small boy who was eager to escape punishment. If the situation hadn't been so terrible, she'd have been amused at his thirty-year-old discomfort.

However, she was anything but amused.

"I probably should go."

No argument there. She didn't answer.

Couldn't.

He let himself out.

Chapter 3

Autumn in New Mexico's foothills smelled of pine and juniper and the terracota earth. The breeze, somewhere between warm and cool, was shoving feathery clouds across the sky. A palpable stillness wrapped itself around the covered porch that stretched the width of Liam Kincaid's modern log cabin. Unless the weather was especially nasty—and it had its moments— he drank his morning coffee in the creaky rocking chair he'd found at a thrift shop, studying the distant Sangre de Cristo Mountains, his bare feet propped on the railing.

No other building in sight. No other people.

Just the way he liked it.

This morning, he was watching his golden retriever snuffling at the base of the trees, checking for overnight intruders. Sadie was always on the lookout for animals—giving them the barking version of *Don't mess with me or my territory*. Three years ago, Liam had found her at the Santa Fe Animal Shelter. Most of the time, she was sweet and curious, slowing down a bit now that her face had more white hair than auburn. Her former owners had trained her to *Sit* and *Come*. Liam had added *No* and *Shut up* whenever she barked too long. Sadie didn't ask much of him, was not put off by his bad moods or having to sit outside the darkroom behind the cabin because the chemicals used to develop black and white film were not good for her.

Liam checked his watch. Nearly nine o'clock. He drank the last of the already cold coffee and reached for the leather sandals he wore around the house. "Come on, Sadie. Let's go in. We have company coming."

Edgar Nunez, the Director of Special Exhibits, was driving to Pecos from Santa Fe, where he'd spent last night with his sister. Nunez had called two days ago, asking whether Liam would be interested in doing a major photographic job for the Museum of Northern Arizona. How the Museum had found him Liam wasn't sure, unless it was his photographic exhibit of schoolchildren at Albuquerque's Indian Pueblo Cultural Center last spring. The first time in eight years that he'd displayed any of his work publicly. His recent commissions—few and far between—usually came from individuals or families who wanted a formal portrait to mark a special occasion.

The Albuquerque show had been black and white photos of the twenty-two fourth graders at Aquirre Elementary School. Liam put the show together as a favor to their teacher, Johnny Salas; he and Liam played tennis on the weekends. For four days, Liam prowled Johnny's classroom, trying to be invisible while photographing the children in the classroom and on the playground. What Liam thought of as artistic snapshots. The kids were a mix of cultures and skin colors. A joy to watch and record. Once he finished, he'd spent hours developing the negatives, then printing and matting two sets of 8" x 10" black and white images. Johnny hung one set in the classroom and loaned the other set to the Cultural Center. Working with his camera equipment, old-fashioned by today's digital standards, was the only time Liam felt like himself—his former self.

At 9:40, a faded blue Chevy pickup parked alongside the cabin, and a stocky, dark-haired man, wearing 501 Levi's and a white, long-sleeved shirt with the sleeves rolled just below his elbow, got out carrying a laptop. Too late, it occurred to Liam he should have put on clean Levi's and found something other than a much-washed University of New Mexico t-shirt. At least he'd put his sandals on.

He met Nunez at the door with his hand extended. "Hi, I'm Liam. How was your drive?"

"Slow. Santa Fe has more traffic than it used to. I forgot to factor that in."

Once Sadie and Edgar exchanged pleasantries and Edgar had a cup of coffee on the table beside him, Liam asked, "What kind of project are you working on?"

Edgar leaned forward, his face brightening. "We're planning to photograph the Colorado Plateau artists who sell their art and crafts through the Museum shop. Some do business with us only occasionally;

others have been with us for years. We want to honor them by creating a permanent gallery in the Museum. This will be the first phase. We've also made arrangements with a major gallery in New York City to debut the photos in late April next year before we have our showing here in the fall. That gives us about five months to put together the photographs. The Museum will be fitting out a studio in one of our empty offices with whatever lighting and back drops you need. Having the artists come to the Museum is much more efficient than you driving all over the Plateau.

"Everything is in place. All I need is you signing on to do the photography. We'd like you to take black and white 4" x 5" negatives. We're thinking of enlarging them to 24" x 30" before framing."

Liam licked his lips nervously and took a careful breath, "I, ah, don't do major projects like that."

"You did."

Past tense. The Museum had done its homework.

He nodded.

Edgar leaned forward again. "We've researched you. You're very good. One of the best. Photographers of your caliber aren't easy to come by. We'll pay you top price. Provide whatever you need to get the job done."

Liam's knee jerk response was *No—no way.* He'd deliberately chosen to stay below the commercial radar, avoiding the temptation to take on big commissions or enter the digital world. He stayed away from social media, didn't have a website. He worked when he wanted. Like the children's pictures for Johnny. Letting customers find him.

Again, "Does the project interest you?"

Liam cleared his throat. "I'm not really doing much photography anymore."

In spite of Liam's answer, Edgar sensed he had piqued his interest. "So far we've chosen fifty-seven individuals; you'll be photographing thirty right now. Then do a second round late next year. I'm assuming you'll want to develop the film yourself. A small, high-quality professional lab in Sedona has agreed to do the final printing under your supervision. We'll arrange for the matting and framing to meet the New York gallery's guidelines. Would our timeline fit your schedule?"

"I rarely have a schedule."

The children had been Liam's biggest project since moving to Pecos. One of the reasons he'd chosen Pecos was its isolation. Fewer than two thousand people surrounded by wilderness, yet only half an hour from Santa Fe. An hour from Albuquerque. Familiar territory. He'd grown up in southwestern

Colorado and attended the University of New Mexico before transferring to the New York Film Academy. With the money from the sale of the New York apartment, he bought this wooded acre and ordered a modular, one-story, cabin with massive windows to take advantage of the scenery. The cabin was a half mile from the nearest paved road, not easy to find, even with a GPS.

Edgar wasn't willing to let Liam escape. Once more, "Does the project interest you?"

Liam brought himself back to the moment and Edgar's question.

"Which gallery in New York?"

"New Image on the Upper West Side."

Liam remembered that it had a topnotch curator who might remember him.

Though he wanted to resist Edgar's proposal, the possibility of recording faces of Native American artists was intriguing.

After a few minutes, Edgar named the amount the Museum would pay for the job.

Not New York fees, but not an amount to be sneezed at either.

"Can I think it over?"

"Absolutely."

"When do you need my answer?"

"A week from today." Edgar wasn't cutting him much slack.

Liam nodded. "May I have your card?"

Sadie walked them to Edgar's pickup and stood still for one last petting from Edgar. "Where did you find her?"

"The animal shelter in Santa Fe. They didn't have her tied up, and she came right to me as I got out of the car. Sort of like, *What took you so long?* She's all about minding my business. If a dog can be controlling, she is."

Once the pickup was out of sight, Liam pulled Sadie's leash from the hook beside the front door—just in case they encountered an animal that would bring out Sadie's snarky side. "Come on, girl. I need to think."

The news that Jeff's family was moving to Cincinnati took a day or two to really sink in. Kara had been in Flagstaff five months. Only now feeling marginally comfortable. She'd acquired a few casual friends and was learning her new job. Adaptation 101

But now, the principal reason she was living here would disappear as soon as Jeff and Ellen found a place in Cincinnati. Their Flagstaff house already had several offers. Since he'd told her he was leaving, she had not answered their texts or emails. Neither of them had appeared on her doorstep to see if she was okay. Probably wise. Kara was not feeling generous of spirit.

First, Michael abandoned her—*dying probably didn't qualify as abandonment*. Now Jeff, without giving her situation a moment's thought, was leaving her to fend for herself. Angry didn't come close to defining her mood. Her moving here was his idea. For days, she delivered silent rants about his selfishness. Cincinnati? Really? Living most of her adult life in coastal Southern California had spoiled her for almost any other part of the country. Flagstaff's weather was difficult enough. There were days she'd give anything for a whiff of salt air and the whoosh of waves pushing onshore.

Most important, moving to Cincinnati was not a financial option. She couldn't keep chasing his family across the country, expecting them to keep her in their lives.

Though Jeff's departure was common knowledge in the city, only Maddy asked what Kara was going to do. Their paths crossed on a Wednesday when Kara was returning a book on Navajo rugs to the Museum's library.

"I saw the article in the *Sun* last week—about your son's new job—will you be following him?"

Kara sighed, "I can't afford to, even if I wanted to, which I don't."

"Did you have any warning about his plans?"

Kara shook her head. Even if she'd known, her input wouldn't have mattered. Jeff took his career very seriously. That acorn didn't fall far from the father tree.

"I'm so sorry."

"Not nearly as sorry as I am."

An elderly couple came into the lobby, and Maddy turned to greet them.

Kara let her anger fester. Telling Jeff how angry she was wouldn't change what was happening. She probably shouldn't burn a bridge she might need someday, but she wasn't quite ready to end the pity party she was indulging in.

The silence was broken when Ellen and the twins appeared at Kara's front door on a Sunday afternoon.

Ellen was hesitant. "Can we come in?" She looked weary, dark circles beneath her eyes.

Kara smiled and stood aside so they could enter.

Molly hugged her Nana's legs. "Why haven't you come over? I miss you."

Kara knelt down. "I've missed you guys too."

Jared hung back until Kara reached out to bring him into their hug. "There are apples on the kitchen counter. Choose one each."

Ellen sat tentatively on the edge of the sectional. Kara took the rocking chair, facing her daughter-in-law, listening to the twins chatter as they were deciding which apples to choose.

Ellen cleared her throat. "Are you mad at us? You haven't answered any of our messages."

Kara took her time answering, debating the degree of honesty that was necessary. "Mostly mad at Jeff."

"He didn't do this intentionally."

Ellen's defense of her husband was part of the Code of Wifely Support. Kara had engaged in it more than she'd like to remember, especially when Michael missed a holiday dinner or a birthday celebration. *He really wanted to be here, but—*

Ellen stood up. "Don't take it out on the kids."

"I don't intend to."

"I really came over to tell you in person that I'm two months pregnant. It's not the kind of news that should be in an email."

A new grandchild half a continent away. Kara couldn't decide whether to be gracious or silent. Silent won.

Ellen picked up her purse and called to the children. "Come on you guys. We need to go home."

Kara wasn't especially proud of her behavior with Ellen. A bit late for a redo.

Two days after Ellen's visit, Kara received a call from Michael's partner, Adam, asking whether she could come to LA for a couple of days. "I'm planning a change in the firm, and I'd like to discuss it with you. My treat.

You can probably use some California sunshine. Brooke will meet you at the airport."

It was an easy *yes*. She needed something to take her mind off Jeff's defection.

Adam forwarded the flight confirmation number and itinerary, Phoenix to LAX, and the name of a hotel. She only had to pay for her meals.

Before leaving, she alerted her longtime friend Beth, who still lived in Kara's old neighborhood, that she would be in town. Kara needed someone to unload on, and Beth was a good listener. They had met when Beth's daughter and Lindsay were lifeguards at Manhattan Beach the summer before their junior year in high school.

When she landed in LA, the temperature was 72—Flagstaff was a chilly 56. No need for the jacket she was carrying as she entered the terminal. Thank goodness she'd also packed a cooler outfit, just in case.

From LAX, the drive to the Pier Inn in Redondo Beach, two blocks from the law office, took nearly an hour. The evening commute turned the 405 into a parking lot. LA was even more congested and intense than she remembered. In the months since she'd left LA, she'd obviously become accustomed to Flag's slower pace. Thank goodness she wasn't driving.

Brooke dropped her off at the hotel entrance. "Adam scheduled your meeting for 9:30 tomorrow. Will that be okay?"

"Sure. Thanks for meeting me."

"Will you need a ride?"

"No thanks."

The law firm was a pleasant walk in the 70 degree sunshine. Adam kissed her cheek and handed her coffee. "You look well."

"I am."

They settled in the small conference room with coffee and freshly baked croissants; Adam remembered her preferences. They chatted about his family and hers. Small talk before his news.

"I wanted to tell you in person that I've asked Calvin Farmer to come into the firm as my partner." When Kara didn't respond, he continued, "I can't handle all the work by myself, and he's agreed to pay off what I owe you for your half of the firm. Instead of a monthly payment, you'll have the lump sum to invest. Are you still in touch with Michael's financial guy at Merrill Lynch?"

"Yes." There would be no more interest attached to the payments. More unexpected change. Why couldn't the world stay still long enough for her to get comfortable?

"Good, then he'll be able to help you decide how best to invest it for the long term."

Kara wasn't totally surprised by Adam's news. Paying for her trip to LA had telegraphed something was up. "When should I expect the money?"

"January first. Easier to start at the beginning of the tax year."

It was time to be gracious. "Michael would approve of your choice. He liked Calvin."

As soon as she returned to her hotel room, she called Merrill Lynch to make an early morning appointment. She needed a plan that would give her—for the time being— the same monthly income she'd been getting from Adam.

When Beth Middleton picked her up for an early dinner at Tony's on the Pier, Kara's head was still processing Adam's information. Studying the waves reflecting the last of the sunset, she sighed, "I truly miss the ocean."

Beth licked the salt on the edge of the glass holding her Margarita, then "Do you miss the traffic too?"

"No." Kara sipped her own Margarita. "Umm, so good. I haven't had one of these since we were here the last time."

"I'm not a fan of Phoenix. Is Flagstaff better?"

One thing Kara liked about Beth was her directness. No need to wonder what she was thinking.

"Plenty of trees and hills. Skiing not far from town. Definitely cooler and smaller than Phoenix. A much slower pace than LA. However, I'm going to have to buy snow tires because Flagstaff is almost seven thousand feet and eventually there will be a real winter. I've never lived through a winter before."

"How's the family? The twins must be, what? Five?"

"They'll be five in November—about the time they move to Cincinnati." Kara struggled to keep her voice even.

The surprise evident on Beth's face made Kara feel a little better about her own reaction to their move.

"They're leaving and you're staying?"

Kara nodded.

"Jeez! What did you say?"

"I haven't talked to Jeff since he told me. What I'd like to say might ruin our relationship permanently. I've been skyping with the children. And Ellen is pregnant again."

"Are you thinking of moving back to California? Is that why you're here?"

"No. I can't afford to. I came because Adam wanted to talk to me. He's bringing in a new partner and paying off the note I hold on the practice. He wanted to tell me personally. He's always careful about such things."

Their food came and Kara encouraged Beth to talk about herself and her family. Talking about Jeff decamping to the Midwest would not improve the lovely chicken parmesan she'd ordered.

Over dessert, Beth found more questions. "Are you making friends?"

"Here and there, mostly at the Museum where I'm working on the weekends. I'm still the new old lady on the block."

"You're not old and I'm not old. Any interesting men?" Beth had been divorced for five years.

"Of course not."

"It's been two years, my friend. You don't have to stay celibate forever. If Michael were on his own, he'd probably have remarried by now."

There were times when Beth's directness was uncomfortable but, in this instance, she was probably right.

"The whole idea of dating is—" Kara couldn't explain. "And going on a dating website just seems wrong."

After dinner, they browsed the shops on the Pier like they'd done many times before. Something else that was the same but not, since she couldn't afford to buy anything.

The next afternoon, Brooke drove Kara to LAX for the flight back to Phoenix. Kara bought a sandwich in the Phoenix airport, retrieved her car from the long-term lot, and drove up the Black Canyon Highway to Flagstaff.

What passed for home.

Chapter 4

Michael died on a Tuesday in early November. By the following Tuesday, Kara felt like someone had tossed her into the middle of a deep lake and yelled, *Swim!* Yet no matter how hard she swam, she couldn't reach the shore.

She arranged Michael's memorial service, wrote the obituary notice, and notified family and friends of his death. Awkward, stressful phone calls.

No time to grieve or rail at the unfairness of it all.

Fortunately, Adam was the executor of Michael's will and living trust. When the two friends opened the law office, they'd set up similar trusts, each naming the other as executor, the surviving partner agreeing to buy out the other's half of the business over a period of five years. The amount of paperwork for the transfer of title and removing Talmadge from all aspects of the business took months. Michael had put his heart and soul and time into the practice, too often stealing time from their personal life, and now his legal fingerprint had been erased. A life lesson was in there somewhere.

Dying required an incredible amount of documentation. Every time she turned around, she had to provide someone with a death certificate. There was the paperwork for Michael's IRA account and mutual funds, name changes, other changes and more changes. At some point, Kara almost—almost—stopped paying close attention to what she was signing.

Jeff and Lindsay came for the memorial service. Ellen remained in Flagstaff because the twins had colds. Jeff spent two days consulting with

Adam about Michael's estate, then hurried back to Flagstaff. *Sorry Mom, job, kids, etc. etc.* Lindsay left the day after the service.

Thank God for Adam and the rest of the office staff.

That year, Christmas was a non-event. The world's frenetic holiday cheer only made her feel worse. Kara couldn't find the energy to accept any of the dinner invitations from her friends. She hid out at home, eating whatever she had on hand and, one day, not eating at all. She managed to mail the holiday gifts for Jeff's family and cancel the plane tickets she and Michael had purchased for the trip to Flagstaff over Christmas weekend. And Lindsay didn't call. Kara had always assumed her family would be available in a crisis. Not this time.

In early March, she began to emerge from the emotional hole she'd been living in. Most friends, other than Beth, had stopped calling since she never returned their calls. Adam was the only person she saw regularly because there were still issues in the trust to iron out. Periodically, Kara went to the law office to help the young woman who had taken over her job.

The pieces of Kara's life were strewn everywhere. She hated people feeling sorry for her. Hated feeling sorry for herself. Well-meaning friends told her *Things will get better,* but not until mid-summer did she agree with them. Then, while she was visiting Jeff's family over Labor Day, Jeff proposed she move to Flagstaff.

He presented his case after he'd read the twins their bedtime story. "Your house is bigger than you need. It's something like three thousand square feet with that big yard. Do you still have a gardener?"

"I do and, every two weeks, I have a cleaning lady."

"Those expenses add up."

Kara nodded. Even more troubling, the house was having chronic plumbing problems and a new roof wasn't far off.

So they made lists—Jeff always liked lists—and totaled monthly expenses.

"If I remember my conversation with Adam, the house has about four hundred thousand in equity. With that amount, you could buy something here and have it free and clear. A condo maybe—though you'll still have homeowner's fees and utilities."

By the time she flew back to Jeff's for Thanksgiving, the idea of leaving Torrance had taken root. She and Jeff spent the long weekend looking at Flagstaff's neighborhoods and visiting open houses.

No mortgage or yard and a smaller place to clean. There might even be cash left over to put into a CD. A small financial cushion. She closed on the condo in early February. Her house had sold the previous week.

Downsizing to fit into the condo required getting rid of possessions that had once seemed necessary. Hers and Michael's, Lindsay's and Jeff's. She emailed lists of everything that her children had left in the garage when they went to college, conveniently ignoring them ever since.

"Do you want me to send these to you?"

In Jeff's case, he only wanted his high school annual and a few books, all of which could be moved along with Kara's possessions.

Lindsay, however, wasn't as accommodating. She didn't have room for her keepsakes—everything from dolls to high school pom-poms. The house on the beach was already too small for three people. Her solution: *Just move them to Flagstaff with you.*

Really? The spoiled Lindsay—too often indulged by the entire family so there would be peace—assumed her mother would comply.

Unwilling to cooperate, Kara made an executive/parental decision and shipped the dolls, numerous scrapbooks, and Lindsay's first surfboard to Hilo. The rest went to Goodwill. The odds of Lindsay forgetting the loss of her treasures were not good, but Kara was not moving them to Flagstaff. Taking a stand and getting rid of the clutter was momentarily empowering.

Ironically, seven months after Kara's arrival in Flagstaff, the main reasons for her living here were headed to Ohio. No parenting payoff on the immediate horizon.

Sadie loved riding in the SUV. Liam lowered the passenger-side window part way so she could savor the new smells. Dog paradise. Most of her journeys had been in and around New Mexico, though they'd driven to Pueblo one weekend a year ago. Today, they were on the I-40, crossing Arizona. When Liam called to accept the photographic project, he discovered Edgar wanted him to come to Flagstaff for four or five days so they could set up schedules, and Liam could meet the rest of the Museum staff. They'd begin photographing in January.

"I'll have to bring Sadie. She hates the Doggie Sleepover at the vet's."

"No worry. La Quinta takes pets. I'll have our office manager make a reservation. During the day, Sadie can hang out at the Museum."

And so Sadie was on the road. Her bed, squeaky toys, favorite snacks, and water bowl in the back, alongside the 35mm camera equipment and Liam's duffle. Somewhere around the Petrified Forest, she got bored, curled up on the back seat, and went to sleep.

Liam's first two days working with Edgar at the Museum were surprisingly hectic. Edgar was eager to show Liam everything that was already in place and also asked Liam for suggestions. There were loose-leaf binders detailing the crafts sold in the shop, along with brief biographies and old photos—some were badly faded snapshots. And there were names and faces of the Museum staff to remember. Papers to sign for HR.

Years ago, Liam had been driven by deadlines, some of his own making. For several years now, he had been loping along on a malleable non-schedule. Edgar's schedule came with deadlines. Nevertheless, Liam was finding the project even more compelling than when Edgar had initially explained it. For the first time since his last New York show, eight years ago, Liam was excited about working.

Prior to Liam's arrival, Edgar had spent time visiting a few of the artists' workshops. "I need a sense of how they work and how their creations evolve. It's that intangible element I'd like you to capture. Even though you aren't photographing them in their work space." He pushed his chair away from the desk. "Am I asking too much of the camera?" His intense charcoal eyes held Liam's the same way they had when Edgar was pitching the project in Liam's living room.

"It is possible to capture those kinds of intangibles. I know them when I see them, but I'm never completely sure how they happen. Sometimes the lens is smarter than I am. Like it has eyes of its own."

On Thursday, Edgar and Liam drove to the South Rim of the Grand Canyon to watch a Hopi carver who did weekly demonstrations at the Visitor Center. "We can be a part of the audience, and you can get a feel for how one of our subjects works. He's very good. Bring your 35mm. I have plenty of black and white film."

Flagstaff had already been dusted with snow twice, and Kara was growing accustomed to wearing her heavy coat with a scarf pulled up around her neck. She didn't mind the cold—so far anyway—but she was pretty sure winter hadn't truly set in yet. At least her condo had a good heater.

Every few days, Ellen emailed pictures of the twins and wrote short messages about their new school, about house hunting and how much Jeff liked his job. Kara however was not answering. The family had left with hardly a backward glance and, yes, she was sulking. Perhaps channeling Lindsay, who had always been a grand champion sulker. In hindsight, the foolishness of depending on your grown children to fill your newly empty life was, clearly, stupid. Kara was going to have to learn to fill herself up. If only there were a handbook for leftover parents. The Museum job was saving her. She had a place and a purpose.

When she opened the Museum's front door a little after 8 a.m. Saturday, a bright-eyed golden retriever met her at the door and dashed around her legs, running into the parking lot. Kara flicked on the bank of light switches inside the door, waiting until the fluorescent bulbs kicked in. The lobby was warm, so someone had already turned up the thermostat. On cold mornings, she usually kept her coat on for the first hour or so. Today, she hung it on a hook in the alcove behind the main door.

Curious about who was in the building, she walked into the hall leading to the administration wing. There was a light on in Edgar Nunez's office.

She had only spoken to him once or twice, but whoever owned the dog needed to go after it. She knocked softly on the half-open door.

"Come in." Edgar looked up, "Hi, Kara. Can I help you?"

Seated beside Edgar at a long table strewn with black and white photographs was another man with a shock of dark auburn hair, reading glasses balanced on the end of his nose.

To Edgar: "A dog was in the lobby and ran outside when I opened the Museum door. I couldn't stop it. Is it yours?"

The other man stood quickly, unfolding more height than she expected, "No, she's mine." He dropped his glasses on the table and hurried out of the office.

Kara turned to Edgar, "I'm sorry she got out, but she surprised me."

"It's not your fault. Sadie's been cooped up with Liam and me too much this week. She's probably gone for a run. Liam will bribe her with treats. She won't go far."

Edgar grabbed his down jacket from the peg by the door and followed Liam.

Since they probably didn't need her help, Kara began her usual opening up routine, switching on the computer, setting up the petty cash. She picked up the stack of mail Maddy had left for her and began sorting through it.

Edgar returned in about fifteen minutes. "She's on her leash. Problem solved."

"Thank goodness."

"She a great dog. Liam lives on an acre near Pecos, so she's used to having room to run."

"Pecos? Is that in Arizona?" She really needed to get a state map and learn more about the area.

"New Mexico. A little east of Santa Fe."

He returned to his office and a few minutes later Liam, with Sadie on a leash, reentered the lobby. Kara came from behind the counter. "Hi, Sadie," and reached down to stroke her head. To the tall owner, "I'm glad you caught her before she got into the street."

"I didn't catch her; she's way too fast for me. I just got a few of her treats from the car and started walking. Works every time. She knows I'll get treats to woo her back. She has a devious side."

"She's beautiful."

His smile came slowly but was worth the wait. "I'm sorry, did Edgar say your name was Carol?"

"Kara Talmadge. I do Maddy's job on the weekends."

"Liam Kincaid. I'm working on a project with Edgar."

"Is that what the photographs are for?"

"Yes. Come have a look."

She didn't have to open the Museum for another fifteen minutes so she followed him into Edgar's office.

As they walked in, "Let's see what Kara thinks of the pictures. A third opinion."

"Good idea." Edgar stepped aside to make room for Kara. On the table were nine 8" x 10" black and white prints. Five were portraits of a thirtyish Native American man. Shoulder-length black hair pushed behind his ears. The sharp planes of his face gave him a regal look. The other photos showed his hands carving what looked like a figure of some sort. The camera had caught the hands and wood and knife at various angles.

"They're beautiful. I love the carving pictures. Who is he?"

Edgar answered. "Joe Takala. He's Hopi, from Second Mesa, and that's the beginning of a Kachina doll. We sell his work in the shop."

Liam picked up one of the carving photos. "The lighting at the demonstration wasn't good. When I have the right lighting, they'll be better." He turned to Kara, "We're trying to decide whether to stick with just portraits or add a smaller picture with the artist's hands carving or weaving."

Kara glanced at her watch, "I need to open up." Over her shoulder, "I think the hands add a lot." Walking back to the lobby, she regretted throwing in her opinion. What did she know about photography? She definitely needed to Google Hopi, Second Mesa and Kachina.

The next day, Liam and Sadie returned to Pecos, promising Edgar they'd be back in Flagstaff the first week of January to start work. Liam needed to make arrangements for his mail to be forwarded to the Museum and for his friend Johnny Salas to check on the house when he had time. Making the five-hour drive from Flagstaff to Pecos during the winter would be difficult if there were storms. Liam and Sadie would be staying in the cabin that the Museum used for visiting dignitaries or, in this case, the photographer for Edgar's project.

Besides packing personal items, he loaded lab equipment and lights, along with the stands and umbrellas he would need in the Museum studio. Though the professional lab in Sedona would be doing the finished prints, Liam would still do the initial developing. Edgar had already requisitioned 4" x 5" and 35mm black and white film and the developing chemicals. Everything would arrive about the time Liam returned to Flagstaff.

Christmas morning, he called his older sister Tracy in Raleigh, North Carolina, to wish her Merry Christmas and tell her he would be in Flagstaff until mid-April. Though they hadn't seen one another in almost two years, they talked every few weeks.

"The project sounds interesting. Are you taking Sadie?"

"Of course. She's my soul mate."

"Not funny, Lee. It's time you went looking for a human one."

"Had one."

"There's no rule that you can't have two."

He changed the subject. "How are the boys?"

"Nick is still obsessed with soccer. It would be better if he were obsessed with graduating. He might have to go to summer school. Al, fortunately for our budget, is living off-campus, sharing an apartment with two friends. They'd both love to see you."

"Maybe when this job is done."

"I'm glad you're working."

"I'm glad you're glad. Give Seth my best."

Chapter 5

The third Christmas without Michael.
Hard in a different way from the first two. Then it was Michael's absence that hovered over the season. This year the twins were in Ohio, so she had to be satisfied with seeing them on a screen on Christmas morning. No hugs. The children were changing so fast. Molly's hair was long enough for a ponytail. Both looked taller. They had adopted a dog. Part poodle, part unknown.

"Nana, when are you coming to see us? We have sleds and we're going to have a baby brother."

"I don't know when I can come." Adjusting to the cold in Flagstaff was enough for now. No sense going to Cincinnati, which already had a foot of snow on the ground. Someone had told her it was 71 degrees in Torrance. No wonder LA freeways were often at a standstill.

Lindsay called on Christmas night to thank Kara for the Amazon gift card and to mention ever-so-casually that she had a new address because she was now living with her boyfriend.

Boyfriend?

Lindsay hadn't talked about anyone special. But then Lindsay wasn't good at sharing, and Kara couldn't check her daughter's Facebook page since she didn't have a Facebook account of her own.

"What's his name?"

"Max."

Surely he had a last name. Pulling information from her daughter was never simple. "What does he do?"

"He teaches surfing. He's a world class surfer." With Lindsay, answering two or three mother-questions was usually her limit so, for the third question, Kara chose to ask for the new address.

Lindsay rattled it off before Kara could find a pen. "I've gotta go, Mom. Love you. Merry Christmas."

The surf was probably up. Some parents couldn't get their grown children out of the house. Kara couldn't keep hers in the same time zone.

The day before Liam and Sadie were due to close up the house in Pecos and drive to Flagstaff, Edgar called. "I'm in the hospital."

"What happened?"

"I encountered a tree while skiing at Snowbowl. I'm at St. Joseph's in Phoenix. Tomorrow the doctors are going to operate to put my right leg back together with plates and pins. They make it sound like an engineering project. I may never get through airport security again."

"Is the project off?" Liam was surprised at his disappointment. He'd begun to look forward to working with Edgar. To being immersed in the artistic side of photography.

"No, nothing like that. I've already made all of the studio appointments, and the arrangements are in place for the New York show. However, you might be on your own while working at the Museum. I've talked to Chet Repik, the assistant director, and he's looking for someone to help you during the project—until I can get back. Except for the next few days, you can call me if you need to. You know what's in the binders, and the appointment calendar is on my computer in the Photo Project folder. My office computer password is written inside the front cover of the blue binder."

They talked about what alterations had already been done in the studio and the makeshift lab behind the Museum and who to contact for the key to the cabin.

When the call ended, Liam looked over at Sadie, who was enjoying the handful of ice cubes he'd put in her bowl. "Well girl, guess we're on our own for a while." Oddly enough, he wasn't bothered by the turn of events. Maybe a sign that he was ready to take a small step forward, instead of moving sideways or going in circles. He'd figure things out once he got back to Flagstaff.

Kara had been trying to ignore the fact that Flagstaff would eventually get a big snowstorm and she would need snow tires on her car. Another major expense.

She'd recently invested in a down jacket and lined boots. *A Christmas present to myself.*

Her living expenses were less than in California but that didn't keep her from worrying about money, especially since Adam's new law partner would be paying off the note for the law firm ahead of schedule. Until now, she hadn't needed to touch her principal, but the part-time job at the Museum only covered the day-to-day expenses like gas and groceries. She needed a second job.

She worked up her courage to talk to the owner of The Art Depot, being sure to mention she'd been an art major. The conversation with the owner, Edith Osca, was pleasant, but the store didn't need more help. Edith and her daughter, plus a part time art student from Northern Arizona University, handled the retail end of the business. Her husband did the ordering and bookkeeping. No opening there.

She went online to see whether there was an employment agency in the city. There were three. If she was going that route, she'd need to put together a *c.v.* Showing up at an interview without one would confirm her amateur employee status. What if she couldn't find a job, even a job in the world of claustrophobic cubicles? Her computer skills had been sufficient for Michael's office, but his programs were old. Perhaps she needed to enroll in a computer class at the community college. Working as a waitress would be her last job choice, but it might come to that. She'd never been able to carry a full cup of coffee without spilling some into the saucer.

Michael, this is your fault.

On the same day she printed out her *c.v.*, she received a call from Chet Repik at the Museum, asking her if she could meet him at ten o'clock the next morning.

Oh swell. I'm going to be fired.

Chet was stocky, maybe 5' 7" or 8". Receding hairline, thick glasses. "Nice to see you again, Kara. Help yourself to coffee." He was holding a mug. A battered Mr. Coffee Maker was on a small table. "Sorry about the powdered cream. I don't have a refrigerator."

Kara poured coffee into a mug, added the powdered cream, and sat in the chair across the desk from him.

"I'm glad you could come in. Maddy tells me you're enjoying your weekends in the lobby."

Kara nodded, then murmured, "Yes."

This didn't feel like she was being fired.

"I'm sure you're wondering why I asked you to come in. We have an emergency situation. Do you know Edgar Nunez?"

"Yes, I've met him."

"He had a skiing accident a few days ago and will be on medical leave for several weeks. He's been laying the groundwork for a project with Liam Kincaid, photographing a group of the Native American artists who sell their work through our shop. With Edgar sidelined, Liam will need someone to help keep the appointments on schedule and—well—do whatever else needs doing. We want Liam to be free to concentrate on the photography. There'll be some paperwork involved. Maybe errands. Because this is the first time we've done a project like this, we don't know exactly what we'll be encountering." He paused. "Do you think it's something you could handle?"

No hesitation. "Yes, yes, I could."

"Edgar will be available by phone for help if you need it. This job shouldn't interfere with what you're already doing on the weekends. Some days, there might be two or three sittings; some days none. So you would have time off." He smiled. "You'll need to stop by HR to make this official."

"I'll do it today. Thank you" *Snow tires tomorrow.*

He stood up. "Good. Let's go to Edgar's office and look at the material he left. I'll get you a key. Liam will be here sometime tomorrow, and the first photo appointment is Tuesday. Maria Santos, a Paiute basket weaver, who lives near Willow Springs."

Kara set the mug on his desk and followed him out the door. Two jobs, at least for a while.

Because Chet told Kara not to expect Liam until early Friday afternoon, *He has a five or six hour drive,* she took her car into Pep Boys a little after nine. Several people were ahead of her, so she didn't arrive at the Museum until noon.

Maddy smiled as Kara walked into the lobby, "Your new boss was here."

Kara's stomach clenched. "Oh dear, I should have been here. I didn't think it would take so long to change the tires. I forgot about the balancing."

"It's okay. He just stopped by for the key to the cabin near Snowbowl. He'll be back later to unload his equipment. Rather dishy."

Kara relaxed a little. She didn't want to risk losing this second job which, for the time being, was going to keep her from dipping into her savings for things like snow tires. She spent the afternoon studying what Edgar had been doing on the project. Liam Kincaid hadn't returned by the time she left at five o'clock.

Though Liam loved the act of taking black and white photographs— choosing the lighting, angles, and f-stops—developing the film and watching the images magically emerge was the best part. The elective photography class he'd taken his freshman year at the University of New Mexico changed his life. Majoring in Economics couldn't compete. His father, a high school math teacher, was skeptical. *How will you earn a steady paycheck?* The young Liam hadn't cared, in a way still didn't, though at one point he earned more in one year than a math teacher made in five.

Being able to again make photographic magic with his 4" x 5" flatbed camera was what had lured him into taking the Museum offer. He missed the beauty of the process. After picking up the cabin key from Maddy, he and Sadie checked out their temporary quarters, Sadie giving it a thorough sniffing while Liam unloaded everything but the photo gear, then headed back to Flagstaff just as the Museum was closing. Maddy was still on duty—*You just missed Kara*—and took him to the small office that would serve as the photo studio. Then out back to the separate annex, once a storage shed for garden equipment, where Liam could put together a temporary lab so he could work any time of day without setting off the Museum's security system. And most important, none of the chemical odors would seep into the Museum itself.

He was already setting up the lab by the time Kara opened the lobby Saturday morning. He'd left a note scotch-taped to the front door: *I'm working in the annex.* Clearly, he needed a key to the main building. When Betty from the Museum shop came to give Kara a break, she walked to the annex, unsure what he'd expect of her.

In reply to her knock, she heard, "Come in." He was standing on a chair, hanging a large red light from a hook in the wall. She'd forgotten how tall he was, his build more lanky than athletic. He was wearing tennis shoes that had seen better days, faded Levi's and a navy fleece.

She waited until he got down off the chair, then "Sorry I wasn't here when you arrived yesterday." She assumed he remembered who she was.

"No problem."

He seemed to mean it. An almost handsome face, dark eyes and auburn hair that needed a trim. "I'm setting up the lab so I can give everything a dry run before I have actual film sheets to develop. It's a one person job."

"I'm assigned to the lobby today and tomorrow, but I can help with whatever you need on Monday. Where's Sadie?"

"I didn't know what the routine would be on the weekend, so I left her out at the cabin the Museum is providing for us."

Easy to talk about the dog. "Will she be okay in a strange place?"

"Yeah. She's pretty trustworthy, not given to chewing on the furniture. I'll go back soon to take her for a walk. She was cooped up in the car most of yesterday."

"She can hang out in Edgar's office if you want. I have the key."

"Sounds good." He smiled, a rather enigmatic smile that she could get used to. Maddy was right, *Dishy*.

Chapter 6

When he accepted Edgar's job offer, Liam hoped the malicious ghosts that had stolen his love of photography had, after all this time, been laid to rest. Photographing Johnny's students hadn't attracted the memories but this morning, as he was loading the 4" x 5" film holders for Maria Santo's portrait, he felt his chest tightening. Not a good sign. The panic attacks always came unannounced. He stopped what he was doing. Forcing himself to take deep, even breaths.

"Maria's here." It took him a moment to realize the voice belonged to Kara—not Ariane. Liam moved away from the camera, forcing himself to extend his hand and smile at Maria, who was carrying a jacket and pulling a rolling case containing her basket weaving materials. Probably in her late thirties, her long, black hair brushed off her face, falling below her shoulders. She was wearing faded jeans; her blouse was a coarse white cotton with elaborately embroidered flowers along the neckline. Perfect for a headshot.

Her voice was low and smooth, "Where should I put the baskets?"

Liam had found a much-scrubbed pine table in one of the Museum's storerooms. "Let's set everything out here."

While Liam and Maria positioned the completed basket covered with elaborate red beading and the incomplete basket Maria would be weaving for the photo, Kara rolled Edgar's desk chair just inside the studio door. If Liam needed something during the shoot, she could easily leave. She was at once apprehensive and excited. A performance of sorts was about to begin.

By eleven o'clock, Maria was seated on the chair placed within the circle of umbrella-shaded lights. Its straight back low enough not to show in the photo. Liam spent an hour trying various camera angles and arranging the lights and umbrella shades, as Maria's head turned this way and that. Through it all, Maria was relaxed, but Liam was still trying to shake the tension in his chest. When he was satisfied with the set up, he took several profile shots and one straight on, with her looking directly into the lens, *As though you were looking into a person's eyes*, then a couple of shots halfway in between. Maria was an amazingly photogenic subject, with an angular bone structure that captured the light and shadows.

Liam finished a little after noon. "Kara, would you turn on the room lights?" He switched off the lights beneath the umbrellas. "Maria, before we work on the baskets, you probably should walk around for a bit. You've been sitting still for a while."

"I'm fine. Where's the rest room?"

Kara opened the hall door. "I'll show you."

While they were gone, Liam changed the lighting, lowered the tripod so the head was level with the table, and unscrewed the 4" x 5" camera. The special close up lens on the 35mm Nikon would allow him to get closer to the basket Maria was weaving. He wanted the focus to be on her fingers, perhaps freeze the blur of their intricate movement.

Maria declined Liam's lunch invitation. "Thanks, but my sister's expecting me. Will I get to see the proofs?"

"As soon as I have contact sheets, Kara will give you a call."

"Where's Edgar?"

Kara explained about the skiing accident and surgery. "He's doing well but will need another operation, then rehab for a few more weeks."

When Liam returned from walking Maria to her car, Kara was at

Edgar's desk, scrolling through new emails on his computer. "Would you like to get some lunch? I hear Daily Fare has good sandwiches."

She had brought a sack lunch, but joining him would be more fun. "Sure."

Since Michael's death, Kara hadn't shared a meal, one-on-one, with a male other than Jeff or Adam. Sitting across the table from Liam was surprisingly comfortable. Small talk about Maria's photos and tomorrow's appointment with the carver Edgar and Liam had visited at the Grand Canyon.

He was easy to talk to. "I've been reading a Heard Museum book on Kachinas. I don't know much about Native American cultures."

The waitress brought their coffee and took their sandwich orders. Kara noticed Liam drank his coffee black, probably something an assistant should know.

"Good idea. I've been away from the Southwest for twenty years, so I've forgotten a lot. I should probably do some research too."

"Did you grow up here?"

"In Colorado, east of Durango. I attended the University of New Mexico in Albuquerque. What about you?"

What about me? Kara was pretty sure he'd think her wife/mother resume was bland.

"Almost two years at UCLA."

"What was your major?"

"Art."

"So you're an artist?"

"Not really. I dropped out to get married and have a family. I never went back."

"Do you sketch or paint now?"

"Sometimes." She'd tried to interest Jeff and Lindsay in art, tried teaching them the basics, but neither was interested. "But it's bit late to start again."

Their orders arrived. Huge hamburgers. Kara would be taking half of hers home for dinner. Liam had no trouble polishing off all of his.

After that first day, whenever they had a morning photo shoot, they ate lunch at Daily Fare. Sometimes the artist joined them, sometimes not. Liam had a quiet way of drawing them out, inquiring about the materials they worked with, how he or she had learned to carve or weave or work silver. Did they have a family?

When Kara and Liam ate alone, he had the same easy way of getting her to talk about herself though, if she asked something about his personal life, he would answer without really answering. He was okay with questions about Sadie or Pecos or photography and listened to her anecdotes about the twins. *They must miss you.* When she asked whether he had children, a firm *No.*

Working with him was fun as well as educational. As the days passed, she gradually learned to anticipate what he would need at various stages during a shoot, what the subjects might want, and enjoyed talking to the artists, keeping them occupied while Liam readjusted the lights or the camera. Providing water or coffee or Pepsi or tea. She kept a few snacks in Edgar's office, just in case the shoot ran long.

Later, when Liam was developing the day's film, Kara took Sadie to Edgar's office, twice taking her to the condo when Liam worked past the Museum's closing, anxious to see the results of the day's shoot. Only once did he decide to call an artist back for a do-over.

She learned to recognize when he was frustrated and wisely kept quiet. Sometimes Sadie wandered around the studio and, if he didn't pay attention to her, wandered out into the hallway, obviously bored and a little miffed. Sadie thrived on attention. Occasionally Liam invited Kara to accompany him and Sadie when he went to Sedona to collect the contact sheets or final prints. She was learning a lot about the printing process. How dodging and burning and cropping could improve the original film. Liam seemed to enjoy answering her questions, often supplying more information than she could absorb all at once.

Gradually, the long table in Edgar's office was filling up with folders holding the final 24" x 30" prints. By the end of February, twenty-one of the portraits were complete. March would be busy photographing the final subjects and getting everything framed. Because Liam was becoming more efficient with each sitting, they would easily make the late April deadline. Edgar was planning to be back at work part time in mid-April. The Museum had already sent a few of the finished prints out for framing and would be in charge of shipping everything to the New York gallery.

Kara was making sure the New York program had accurate information on each of the subjects. She and Liam would do the final proofing.

She couldn't remember exactly when she began looking forward to seeing Liam. This anticipation wasn't the giddy rush she'd felt when she and Michael began dating. Of course, working with Liam was not dating. She was not looking for a relationship. Being with him quite simply smoothed out the edges of her days. Gave her purpose.

She fell in love with Michael fast and hard. No doubts. No holding back. Because he was clerking for a judge while finishing law school, he had enough cash to send her flowers and take her to upscale restaurants she'd only read about. He was a handsome, confident third year law student; she was a sophomore, still rather naïve about men and certainly about sex. When they began sleeping together, she got a prescription for birth control pills but, while her body was adjusting to the pills, they were no longer needed. Jeffrey Michael Talmadge had already been conceived.

When she told Michael about the baby, he didn't bat an eye. Was excited about being a father. *We'll get married now. It's just earlier than we planned.* Michael's parents were divorced, his father at a diplomatic post in Nigeria, his mother remarried and living in Costa Rica. *They probably wouldn't be able to come to the wedding.* Kara's parents, living in San Jose and imagining a "real" wedding for their daughter, were less than pleased when Kara called to tell them she and Michael had eloped to Vegas. Her mother, sensing there was more to the story, asked "Are you pregnant?" When Kara confessed, "What about college?" At that point in her life, Kara didn't care about staying in school. She was in love and beginning to plan for the baby.

Joyous moments. Eons ago.

The morning the Museum cabin's water heater rusted through, creating a small lake in the kitchen and bathroom, Liam left a message on Kara's voicemail: *I'll be late. Keep Nastos occupied until I can get there.* Then he called the Museum's business office to ask how they wanted to handle the problem. The rusty water certainly needed to be pumped out soon, and fans installed to help dry everything as much as possible. He packed up whatever he and Sadie would need for a few days and abandoned the cabin, which until now had been quite comfortable as a home away from home.

He arrived at the Museum an hour late, a little preoccupied but in good humor. "Fortunately, Sadie woke me up when the water started seeping into the bathroom so I could get the water heater turned off before the entire cabin was flooded." Turning to Nastos, who was drinking his second cup of tea, "I'm sorry to keep you waiting."

"No problem. Kara has been most kind. And I had time to walk through the gift shop."

At eighty-one, Nastos was legendary in the world of Navajo silver. Liam had been looking forward to photographing him. Probably the oldest of their subjects, his face was leathery, etched with fine lines that, under the lights were incredibly beautiful. Not a word typically applied to men of a certain age. Liam spent longer than usual on this portrait and the 35mm shots of him polishing an elaborate, turquoise-studded belt buckle. Liam already had a sense that one of these headshots might be the signature piece of the collection. Perhaps a candidate for the program cover.

Liam didn't finish until almost two o'clock. Because he knew they'd be running late, he'd sent Kara out for sandwiches for the three of them. As Liam was packing up the cameras, Maddy leaned into the studio: "Chet has somebody scheduled to go to the cabin around three o'clock. If it's as bad as it sounds, you shouldn't stay there. He's worried about mold and other evil things. Sorry, I need to get back to the lobby," and she disappeared.

When Kara returned from walking Nastos to his truck, Liam was sitting on the chair the artist had vacated, rubbing Sadie's head, which was propped on his thigh. "The cabin has been declared a health hazard. I guess it's back to the motel."

"I have a spare room in my condo." Had she actually said that? "It has its own bathroom."

"Are you sure? Sadie might be more than you want."

"Sadie's been there a few times while you were working late. It won't be strange for her."

Having you there may be the strange part. Good strange.

He smiled—she was learning to like that smile. "We accept—at least for tonight."

On the surface, a simple solution to an unexpected need. She'd just asked a forty-something man to stay in her guest room. A man who was sort of her boss. Mostly still a stranger.

While Liam was in the lab developing the day's film, Kara was at Edgar's desk, making a grocery list, trying to decide whether she should go home early to make sure the guest bathroom was clean.

Chapter 7

Replacing the water heater and drying out the cabin floors took longer than anyone expected. A week after the flood, Liam was still occupying Kara's spare room with no estimate from the clean up crew of a completion date.

Kara was rather enjoying the arrangement. Liam made it clear she didn't need to feel responsible for feeding him or looking after Sadie. The first night, because it was after seven when he finished developing the day's film, he picked up pizza on the way to her condo. Kara provided salad and wine. He helped clean up the kitchen, then took Sadie for a walk. Michael always thought kitchen chores were beneath his pay grade.

The next night, Kara joined them on their walk, and the third night she and Liam collaborated on fixing dinner. He made chicken fajitas and she again fixed a salad. She was discovering he was a good cook, not afraid of herbs and sauces. One day, when there was no photo shoot scheduled, they went to the grocery store together, then spent the afternoon experimenting with a filo dough recipe. Neither of them mentioned his moving to the motel.

One night, they ate at Northern Pines and caught the last showing of *The Darkest Hour,* sharing a rather large bucket of popcorn. By the time they got home, Sadie was in a major sulk. She wasn't used to being left behind.

Though Kara loved having Liam and Sadie in her house and loved working on the photo project, they were almost finished. Only five more artists to be photographed, and the finished prints were piling up in Edgar's office. Ten days after the flood, Chet told Liam the cabin had been cleared for occupancy.

The next morning, Liam was up earlier than usual, packed the SUV, fixed himself coffee, and took Sadie for her walk. When he came back, a blonde, very tan young woman in cotton slacks and a t-shirt was waiting on the front porch, shivering in the 40 degree cold.

"Can I help you?" He put Kara's spare key in the lock and opened the door.

"I must have the wrong address. Is this 221?"

"Yes. Who're you looking for?"

"Kara Talmadge. I'm her daughter."

"This is her place. Come inside. You look cold."

"She didn't answer when I rang the bell."

"She's probably in the shower."

"Who are you?" Straight to the point.

"Liam Kincaid. I've been staying here until a plumbing problem is fixed at my place. Actually, I'm leaving today." He let Sadie off the leash and she made a beeline for her water bowl, still on the floor in the kitchen.

"Lindsay?" Kara hurried into the living room, drying her hair with a towel. "I heard your voice. When did you get here?"

"Just now. I drove up from Phoenix. Your—*friend*—let me in." Impossible to miss the disapproval in her voice.

Refusing to take Lindsay's bait, Kara stopped drying her hair. This was not the best way to introduce Liam to a member of her family. Her daughter was all-too-capable of putting her on the defensive. "Why didn't you let me know you were coming?"

Recognizing the tension in the room, Liam escaped into the kitchen to allow Kara and her daughter privacy. "It's time for us to get out of here, Sadie." After rinsing out her water bowl, he put Sadie back on her leash and walked into the living room. "We need to check out the cabin. Nice to meet you, Lindsay." To Kara, "I'll see you at work," and made his exit.

Kara was sorry to see him go—for a couple of reasons. One: she'd enjoyed his company and two: she was going to have to deal with her daughter one-on-one. Lindsay had never been an easy child—always asserting her independence, often distancing herself from her family.

"So can I stay until Sunday? Since he's leaving."

"Yes. And his name is Liam."

"Which room?"

Kara led her to the spare room, grateful that Liam's sheets and towels were piled by the door and the bed had been freshly made up. Dishwashing and bed making. He'd obviously lived alone for a while. She left Lindsay in the bedroom while she took the laundry into the small alcove off the kitchen, stuffed everything into the washing machine, and turned it on.

A few minutes later, a barefooted Lindsay padded into the kitchen. "Any cereal? I'm famished. Why don't they serve food on airplanes?"

Kara opened the cupboard next to the sink. "There's plenty of cereal—2% milk in the fridge." Instead of having cereal, Kara fixed herself toast and turned the Keurig on. She voted not to ask questions yet. Pushy mother tactics only made her daughter back off. Whatever had moved Lindsay to spend money on a ticket to Arizona and a rental car would come out eventually. Kara had time. There was only one artist coming in today at 11:00.

They ate in silence, Lindsay devouring two bowls of cereal while Kara drank two cups of coffee. Her daughter looked tired, but then she'd been on a red eye flight—six plus hours—and had driven from Phoenix. The fact that she was wearing cotton slacks and a t-shirt suggested she hadn't checked on what the weather would be. The late March temperatures in Flagstaff were very different from those in California or Hawaii.

When Lindsay finished the second bowl, "Is there more coffee?"

"With my Keurig, always, so long as there are pods." This was new. Lindsay had always hated the taste of coffee. Maybe having a new boyfriend had made some changes.

"He's very good looking, your—ah—friend." Kara resisted the temptation to tell her to knock it off. "What does he do?"

"He's a professional photographer. He's doing a series on Native American artisans for the Museum of Northern Arizona."

"So what do you do?"

"Manage the details, sort of a go-fer, I guess. The man who created the project broke his leg a week before the work started. I'm filling in."

"Do you like it? Being a go-fer, I mean."

"Actually, yes. No two days are the same." Kara gambled on changing topics: "Are you on spring break?"

"Yes."

"How was the flight?"

Lindsay looked at her like she'd just asked for an explanation of string theory. "Long and cramped." Then adding the non-sequitur of all time, "I'm pregnant."

The earth tipped ever-so-slightly. Kara was sure her face registered shock.

Lindsay was watching her. Then, "No questions? Like aren't you on the pill? Who's the father? Are you keeping it?" Darling daughter in defensive mode, which usually meant she was uncertain but unwilling to admit it. Lindsay wasn't given to sharing much of anything. Not until she'd been accepted at the University of Hawaii did she tell her parents that she'd applied for and received a scholarship.

Truthfully, these were exactly the questions Kara wanted to ask but chose a different tack.

"How far along are you?"

"Three months or so."

"Have you seen a doctor?"

"Of course." Prickly.

While Kara was debating what to say next, Lindsay stood up. "I'm wiped. I need some sleep," and headed for the spare room.

Just as well that Kara was needed at the Museum. Hanging around the house, waiting for Lindsay to wake up and then stonewall her was not what she needed. Trouble was, at some point she would have to return home.

When she walked into the studio, Liam was already setting up the lights around Tacia, a forty-something Zuni woman whose intricate, inlay jewelry was selling for top prices all over the Plateau. "Kara," Liam moved to the table where several pieces of jewelry were lying, "can you go to the shop and ask if they have an extra display stand. I think I'd like to use it for the 35mm shot."

By the time she returned—it had taken the shop salesman a ridiculously long time to find a stand—Liam had finished Tacia's portrait. Once he arranged the finished jewelry on the borrowed stand, the 35mm shot of Tacia polishing one of the larger pieces took only half an hour. It was after one o'clock when the three of them went to lunch.

Later, while Liam was pouring out the developing chemicals in the lab, Kara put Sadie in the car and drove home to see if Lindsay was still sleeping. No such luck. She was wrapped in Kara's white terrycloth robe, watching TV and finishing off a small carton of pecan crunch ice cream.

Sadie dashed to the kitchen and quickly returned as though to say, *What happened to my water bowl?*

"Sorry, girl." Kara found another bowl, ran water in it, then joined Lindsay on the sectional. "Do you want me to fix you something more nutritional?"

Lindsay muted the *Judge Judy* program she was watching. "No thanks, I'm good. So are you renting or did you buy this place?" Proof that Lindsay hadn't paid attention when her mother left LA.

"I bought it. One large house in California for one medium-sized condo in Flagstaff. I came out even. No mortgage."

"It's not too bad."

Damning with faint praise.

"It suits me." *As much as anything does these days.*

"But now Jeff is in Cincinnati."

"True."

"Kinda nervy." She set the empty carton on the glass–topped coffee table.

"It was a good job offer." Kara hadn't meant to defend him, but Lindsay always managed to put her in defensive mode too.

"I think it was a dirty trick."

The most relevant question Kara wanted to ask was *Why are you here?* It would certainly have been cheaper and easier to deliver the baby news via phone. Though Kara was pretty sure she knew the reason, she just wanted Lindsay to verify it. A surprise pregnancy was scary if you weren't married— Kara remembered the feeling. The best way to get the truth from Lindsay was to seem uninterested. Like fishing—she needed to play out the mother-line.

Sadie conveniently filled the conversational gap by planting herself in front of Lindsay, waiting to be petted and admired. Lindsay complied.

"What's her name?"

"Sadie."

"Is she his?"

"Yes. When Liam works in the photo lab, she can't stay with him. The chemicals aren't good for her so, if I'm done at the Museum, I bring her here. He picks her up when he's finished."

"What kind of photography?"

"Mostly he does large format black and white portraits. I understand he's well-known in New York and abroad."

"A cut above iPhone photos?" Lindsay at her most flippant. "So have you looked him up on Google or Facebook?"

"No."

"Aren't you curious? I mean he's been living here." *Subtext: sleeping with you.* Lindsay pulled her phone from the robe's pocket. "Let's see," she tapped and thumbed and scrolled. "No Facebook account. That's weird."

"I don't have one either."

"I offered to set one up for you ages ago but you didn't want it."

An old argument.

More tapping—then reading. "Interesting." Lindsay passed the phone to Kara.

She took one look at the small print and went into the kitchen to find her purse. Sadie followed eagerly, hoping food might be offered. Reading glasses in place, Kara picked up the phone to read the short Wikipedia entry.

Then reread it.

After a few minutes, she returned the phone—wishing Lindsay weren't staring at her. She needed time to digest the information.

"He's not that much younger than you."

"Why does his age matter? I'm just working with him."

"I repeat. He's been living here." Noting her mother's thunderous expression, "Okay, okay. I'll be in the shower."

Liam came for Sadie while Lindsay was showering.

"Just one appointment tomorrow?"

"Yes, 9:30."

"Good. I need to make a run to Sedona afterwards. Want to come? Or do you and your daughter have plans?"

Kara didn't think twice. Going to Sedona or sparring with Lindsay. "I'd love to come."

Lindsay was grateful she'd long ago trained her mother not to ask too many questions. Though she acknowledged Kara's "right" to ask, Lindsay did not handle oversight well. Even from Max. When she was ready to share something, she did. It was a timing thing.

Her mother looked good, maybe even happy. Lindsay was definitely curious about the tall, good-looking Liam with a key to her mother's house. Sunglasses shoved into his hair, killer smile. Was her conservative, rather ordinary mother having an affair? Her mother wasn't bad looking—for her age—her skin still smooth, her hair a mixture of brown and blonde where the gray could hide, neither plump nor too thin.

A mother. Her mother.

Who had a man staying in her house. An unexpected scenario.

Before Kara turned out the light that night, she opened her laptop and pulled up Liam's Wikipedia entry.

Born: 1971, Allison, Colorado.

Education: University of New Mexico, New York Film Academy

Member: Photographic Association of America

Spouse: Ariane Chapin, 2001- 2011

Honors: Photographer of the Year: 2004

A long list of exhibitions and publications. But nothing after 2011.

Puzzling. His professional life had stopped when Ariane was no longer in his life. In spite of her curiosity, Kara felt like she was invading his privacy and exited the site.

She did however intend to invade Lindsay's privacy to get answers about the baby and the absent Max. On Sunday Lindsay was flying back to Hawaii—and they were still dancing all around the pregnancy topic. Kara was low on patience. Once she got to the Museum Saturday morning, she left a text message on Lindsay's cell. **I'm taking you to dinner tonight. Be ready at 5:30.** No asking whether her daughter wanted to go to dinner. Tiptoeing was over. It was interrogation time. Kara was fairly sure it would not be an easy evening, but she did not want her daughter to leave without "the conversation."

Would she keep the baby, put it up for adoption? Marry Max, the surfer-with-no-last-name? Assuming it was Max's. Raise the baby on her own. Or—an option Kara didn't relish—was she planning on moving to Flagstaff? Kara was very sure she would not be moving to Hawaii to help with this grandchild. Then she reminded herself that her daughter was not given to asking for help.

Kara was ever-so-gradually enlarging the borders of her own life. Working with Liam and the photographs had revived the itch to go back to her art. She'd already dug into the boxes of art materials in the garage and started a charcoal sketch of Sadie asleep in Edgar's office. It wasn't all that bad, but she hadn't shown it to anyone. She and Liam had spent one afternoon last month at Walnut Creek National Monument so she could see the cliff dwellings. *My dad took me and my sister when I was about twelve. They're unique.*

She was surrounded by new people that Michael had never known. She wasn't going to let Lindsay pour cold water on this new life, on her friendship with Liam.

When Kara arrived at the condo, Lindsay was dressed in a long, white cotton skirt and lightweight sweater instead of the rumpled chinos and t-shirts she'd been living in since her arrival. And she was on time. Not always something the family had been able to count on. Maybe her daughter was growing up.

Kara had made a reservation at Northern Pines Brewing, the same restaurant she and Liam had gone to. A relaxed ambiance and plenty of comfort food—usually Lindsay's favorite. When they were settled at a table alongside a large window, Lindsay smiled for the first time. "You bring me to a brewery when I'm not supposed to drink."

The baby made its appearance. That would help. "You don't like beer anyway."

"True."

"Have you had morning sickness?"

"A little. Nothing major." She was studying the menu. "Are the steaks good?"

"I had fish but Liam said his steak was good."

"So you and Liam come here?" The same tone as the friend comment.

"Stop that. We came once after we'd been working late at the Museum, and we split the check. It wasn't a date. Sometimes we work late." Why was she apologizing? She was aware however that she didn't mention the movie.

"How'd you get this job? I mean, you told me about the lobby thing, but this is different."

She actually had been paying attention. "They needed someone to fill in at the last minute and I was convenient."

"Does it pay well?"

"It helps. I don't know what 'well' is in this part of the world." And as soon as Edgar returned, she'd be looking for another job.

The waitress took their orders—both chose steaks.

Before she lost her nerve, "Will you keep the baby?"

No hesitation. "Yes."

Kara relaxed a little. A piece of good news. "What about the father?"

"Max."

"Is he on board?"

"I haven't told him yet."

"He's sure to figure it out, you know."

"Before I tell him, I wanted to know how Dad handled it when you told him about Jeff. I mean, you guys weren't married either."

So that was why Lindsay was here. It had taken three days to get to the point of her visit. "In all honesty, your father was excited. We eloped to Vegas a week after I told him."

"Did you ever regret not having a real wedding first and then getting pregnant?"

"Never thought about it. We truly wanted to be together, and Jeff's appearance just moved up the time frame. My parents weren't pleased, however." She paused, "Will Max want to get married?"

"I'm fairly sure he won't. I mean, he loves me and all, but marriage scares him. Maybe it scares me too. When you're married, you always have to consider someone else." Kara decided not to explain that having a child required the same or even more consideration for someone else.

The steaks arrived. Lindsay went after hers as though she hadn't eaten in days, then ordered dessert. Kara put half of her steak in a carry home box, used a latte as dessert, and went after one more issue. "Would you raise the baby alone if you had to?"

Her daughter bestowed one her *Mu-uthe-er* looks. "Max isn't going anywhere. We just won't get married."

Kara didn't comment. Lindsay wasn't really looking for that kind of help. Maybe visiting these few days had, indirectly, provided some sort of support. Hard to tell.

Once Lindsay finished the ice cream sundae, Kara asked, "What time do you need to leave tomorrow?"

"Early. Sixish. My flight is at 10:30."

Kara was encouraged when Lindsay briefly hugged her just before getting in the rental car and driving back to Phoenix. Possibly her daughter's edges had softened a little. She didn't mention Michael's death at all. Didn't talk about Max much. What he was like, how they met. She did have a picture of him with a surfboard. Dusky skin, black wavy hair. Maybe he was Hawaiian or a mixture. Good looking and well built. Beyond that, the baby's father was a mystery. She wanted to ask Lindsay whether she was happy but knew her independent daughter would never reveal such private feelings, certainly not to her mother.

Chapter 8

The Colorado Plateau portraits would be shipped to New York on April 15th.

The New Image Gallery had sent copies of the advance publicity and re-confirmed the delivery date. Details on top of details. Kara dealt with as many as she could but was having to call Edgar several times a day, and twice she hand-delivered contracts to his house for his signature.

He handed her the contract folder: "It's time I get back to work. Crutches and all. I want to take a look at the photos."

Kara was relieved. "Oh good. Liam would really appreciate having another pair of eyes." Even though Edgar had prepared well, they wanted him to verbally approve the work.

He came in on Monday. Kara and Liam had arranged the framed photographs on the floor around the studio walls. Alternating one 24" x 30" portrait with the 9" x 12" photo of the artist working. Each photo was mounted on white archival board and double matted with white archival stock. The metal frames were squared pewter. Standard style for hanging photos in a gallery and, because of their size, covered with plexi-glass instead of glass.

Using his rolling desk chair, Edgar circled the display. Circled again, stopping in front of each photo. Saying nothing. After nearly half an hour, Kara was beginning to worry that he wasn't happy with Liam's work.

Finally: "Superb work, Liam. The directors will be impressed. I'm impressed. And I'm guessing these will impress the New York crowd as well."

Liam smiled slightly, "Thank you."

Kara let out the breath she'd been holding.

After Edgar's wife picked him up, Liam and Kara carried the pictures back to Edgar's office and locked the door.

"I guess that's it, except for the shipping," Liam hesitated, "feels sort of anticlimactic."

Kara nodded. Her part in the project was definitely over. She wished she could attend the New York opening but wasn't willing to spend the money. And no one had offered to pay her way.

"Want to get some dinner?" They hadn't had dinner together since he moved back to the cabin.

"Sure. What about Sadie?"

"I'll take her to the cabin, feed her, and meet you at Northern Pines."

Liam ordered beer and a medium-rare steak, Kara chose wine and salmon.

"The shipping company is scheduled for 9 a.m. tomorrow; can you be there? Edgar's coming too; three pairs of eyes can't hurt."

She was pleased that he still wanted her help. "Of course."

"It'll take several hours."

"No problem." She again had too much free time. Unpaid time.

"Sadie and I are going to Pecos Wednesday morning."

Kara was surprised. He and Edgar were flying to New York from Phoenix the following Tuesday.

To her unasked question, "I need to pick up a decent suit for the reception and a few other things. Wearing sandals and Levi's to a New York opening is not an option."

"While you're in New York, do you want to leave Sadie with me?"

"You wouldn't mind keeping her?"

"Not at all. She's used to the condo." *And me.*

"That would be a big help. I was thinking of asking a friend in Pecos, but Sadie doesn't know him all that well, and she hates staying at the vet's."

"Taking care of her will make me go on walks." It was also a way to stay connected to Liam. After weeks of working together, they had an easy rapport. Sometimes she caught herself hoping there was more than just work involved.

When they reached her car, he opened the door for her, "Would you like to come with us? To Pecos. One day over, one day there to check things out. I have a couple of appointments in Santa Fe and need to get a presentable outfit and a suitcase. Then one day back. You'd be home in time for your weekend shift."

Talk about out of left field.

Why not?

"I'd like that."

In the two hours it took her to get to sleep that night, she re-ran his invitation and her eager acceptance. Nothing implied on either side. She checked to make sure she didn't want implication. Of course she didn't. Fitting into someone else's life or fitting someone into hers, such as it was, would be complicated. In the time Michael had been gone, she'd begun to know herself better, be comfortable in her own skin. No one to please but herself. Pleasing children didn't count. She was glad Liam had invited her and found herself mentally choosing what clothing to take.

She could use an adventure.

They left at dawn Wednesday. Perhaps sensing their destination, Sadie eagerly jumped into the back seat. Liam opened the rear windows enough for her to sniff springtime in the high desert. Every few minutes, Sadie moved between the windows, afraid she'd miss something.

Kara laughed. "Will she finally get tired and lie down?"

"Don't count on it. Sniffing is serious business."

"Does she know where she's going?"

"Oh yeah. It's our fourth trip along this highway."

Like Sadie, Kara couldn't look at everything fast enough. She'd never seen this kind of terrain. It wasn't as barren as the desert in eastern California, the horizon a collage of greens and beiges, none of the colors overly bright. No trees unless there was a town or a ranch house. Not completely flat, an occasional bluff, even some rolling grassland. The Interstate hurriedly by-passed the small towns, skirting the Petrified Forest and Painted Desert. More sky than land, very few clouds. She hadn't imagined there could be so much open space.

Liam couldn't quite explain why he'd invited Kara to Pecos. The rational reasons: Everything about the Southwest was new for her. She was learning what she could from the Museum's library and by talking to the Native Americans Liam was photographing. Experiencing the terrain that fostered much of the Native American art would contribute to her understanding of both the culture and the artists' responses to their unique surroundings. Not until he returned to the Southwest did he discover how much he'd missed its vastness. Everything about New York was vertical. The horizontal of the Southwest suited him better.

The irrational reason for inviting her was that she was easy to be with. She didn't ask the uncomfortable personal questions some women asked: *Are you seeing someone? Are you interested in a relationship?* Trying to ferret out his likes and dislikes.

Discouraging their invasion of his space often took time and, sometimes, outright refusal of their overtures. There were one or two women who had decided he must be gay—certainly not the case—and one or two who had settled for a brief affair—strictly physical—realizing that there wouldn't be more. Kara, on the other hand, didn't seem to want more than companionship.

She had never been on a road trip with a man—other than Michael. Driving across the high desert with Liam felt rather daring. She hadn't told anyone in her family where she was going. If Ellen or Lindsay called—Jeff wouldn't—they would have no way of knowing she was in Pecos. With Liam. They might jump to the wrong conclusion, as Lindsay had. Being a widow—still young by some standards—could be annoyingly awkward. She wasn't publicly wearing widows' weeds, neither was she looking for someone to take Michael's place. She was on *pause*. Rarely looking backward, not planning her future. Simply running in place.

Liam was a relaxed driver, not bothered by silence but, when she did ask a question about something they were passing, he willingly answered. Not too much information, just enough.

Sometime after 3 o'clock, the highway signs began advertising Albuquerque. Liam exited the Interstate at Central and, after negotiating his way into the city, stopped at a Smith's grocery store with a large parking area. "Room to walk Sadie."

While he and Sadie stretched their legs, Kara went grocery shopping. By the time they got to Pecos, still another hour or so, neither would feel much like cooking anything elaborate, so she bought a roasted chicken, a couple of sides from the deli counter and enough staples to last two days. Bread, butter, eggs, and milk, food for Sadie, cold cereal, fruit and a tube of chocolate chip cookie dough. No mixing involved, just baking. She hoped he had pasta or rice.

Once they left the Interstate and wound into the Pecos River Valley, more trees dotted the hillsides, a mixture of pines and aspen just leafing out, not dense enough to interfere with views of the surrounding mountains. More green than they'd seen all day. At a ragged line of rural mailboxes, Liam turned onto a narrow, paved road and, in a few hundred feet, turned again onto a graded dirt road.

"Are we near Pecos?"

"Four miles north. We'll go in tomorrow. I have to touch base with Johnny. He's been coming to the house when he had time to make sure everything is all right."

"And Johnny is?"

"Johnny Salas. He teaches fourth grade in Pecos and regularly beats me at tennis. He and his family have kept me from turning into a full-time recluse." Liam made another turn, this time onto a graveled driveway. "Here we are."

Sadie let out a series of joyous barks.

Kara was surprised that the cabin was so modern and large. She'd been imagining something more rustic, like the Museum's cabin. Instead, she was looking at a light-colored log exterior, a steeply pitched roof, huge windows, and a broad, covered porch.

"It's new."

"Well, yes, three years new. It's modular. They pour a concrete slab, then erect the walls and roof. There's also a shed in the back that I use as a developing lab."

"It's a beautiful area. A long way from everywhere."

"That was what I was after. Come on, Sadie," he got out and opened the back door, "go check it out girl."

Kara got out too, laughing at Sadie's excitement.

"It's bigger than I pictured."

"I'm still amazed how well it turned out. Let's go inside. Sadie'll be on sniffing patrol for a while. She'll come back when she's finished her rounds."

"She won't run away?"

"Not here. Sometimes she goes as far as the mailboxes, but this is home and her food lives here."

The floor to roof windows brought the distant mountains inside. Kara stood in the open doorway. "How wonderful. Inside and outside all at once."

There was a patterned, dark blue couch, two upholstered chairs in front of a medium-sized, flat screen TV mounted on the wall. A large coffee table for the couch, a smaller one between the chairs. Modernistic, arced floor lamps. Laminate floors, no rugs. On the wall perpendicular to the TV were four black and white photographs, about the size of the portraits he'd just finished: Paris at night with the Eiffel tower as the centerpiece, two landscapes, and the portrait of a young, very beautiful woman looking straight at Kara. And as Kara moved further into the room, the woman's eyes followed her. Rather off-putting.

The room was serene, definitely masculine. No sign of a woman's touch, just the portrait.

"Do you have neighbors?"

"The closest is half a mile to the east. This area has been slow to develop; we only have electricity and mail delivery. No natural gas, sewer or city water. I have a well and a septic tank. If the electricity goes out, I have a generator for lights and a wood-burning stove in the kitchen. Because of the vaulted ceiling in here, it's too hard to heat this room without the furnace."

"So you're roughing it."

"Something like that. Let's get the stuff out of the car."

The guest room had the same simplicity and colors as the living room: beige, white and deep blue. She'd packed light, an extra pair of slacks, a couple of long-sleeved t-shirts and toiletries. Her jacket was still in the car. Liam had warned her that, at almost seven thousand feet, the evenings would be cool.

When she returned to the living room, she could see Liam outside with Sadie, throwing a bright red Frisbee. Man and dog playing, Sadie almost tripping over herself in delight. Liam laughing at her. Kara had seldom seen him laugh—sometimes a soft smile, but not out-loud laughter. It changed his face and body language, made him younger, his hair falling over his forehead in spite of his pushing it back.

When Sadie showed signs of slowing down, panting, Liam sat on the bottom porch step and Sadie dropped down in front of him to be petted. He leaned over to rub his hands and face in her fur, talking softly to her.

For an instant, Kara wondered what Liam's hands would feel like.

Unnerved by the thought, she made herself turn away from the window.

Chapter 9

The next morning they drove into Pecos, left Sadie at the dog groomers, and ate breakfast at a hole-in-the wall diner just off the main street. Definitely the local hangout. A retro counter, four booths and large portions of comfort food. Bacon seemed to come with everything. One of the men seated at the counter greeted Liam, asking where he'd been. "I've been working in Flagstaff."

Because his friend Johnny was teaching until mid-afternoon, they went on to Santa Fe. Liam had an appointment with someone at his bank, another with a lawyer, so he dropped Kara off at the beginning of Canyon Road. "Since you're an artist, you'll love wandering through the art shops and galleries." He checked his watch. "I should be finished about one. I'll text you, and we can meet at Café des Artistes, halfway along the road. They have outside seating. If you can't find the restaurant, just ask at one of the galleries. Everyone knows it."

Santa Fe was unlike any place she'd ever been, stucco buildings with protruding wooden vigas, deep patios, and walls smothered in red bougainvillea. Hard to imagine she was still in the States. She leisurely explored the galleries, art studios, and gift shops—then met Liam for lunch, eating street tacos and drinking beer in the shade of an orange umbrella. Liam listened as she talked about the sculpture studio where she'd spent an hour. Before returning to Pecos, they walked back to the studio to look at the sculpture she'd been describing during lunch. The artist was working on a large block of brown soapstone, gradually coaxing a woman's face from the raw stone, her hair extending to one side as though blown by the wind.

As they were walking to the car, Liam remarked, "Too bad he's not Native American. We could put him in the portrait project. I would love to photograph his hands holding that chisel."

They caught up with Johnny in his classroom, cleaning up after a day of energetic fourth graders. "Hey stranger. About time you showed up." They hugged briefly.

"Johnny, this is Kara Talmadge. She's been assisting me at the Museum. This is her first trip to Santa Fe. She spent the morning in the galleries on Canyon Road."

She and Johnny shook hands. "And I loved every bit of it, though I'll admit I barely saw half of the shops."

"Too much to absorb in one day. It needs to be taken in a little at a time. You must come back." He moved his desk chair toward Kara. "Take my chair. Liam and I will perch on the little people chairs." To Liam, "Did you go to the Post Office?"

"I did and extended the forwarding for another thirty days. Thanks for checking on the house." Liam asked about Johnny's family and some of the people they played tennis with.

Johnny was slightly shorter than Liam, wiry, richly black hair cropped short. He had a cheerful look even when he wasn't smiling. His students probably loved him. The classroom was inviting, lots of color, a grouping of chairs around a table with a *Let's Read* sign in the middle, a long art table on one side, and the usual individual desks arranged in a half circle instead of the formal rows Kara remembered from her days in elementary school.

After a few minutes, Johnny turned to her, "Are you going to New York too?"

She shook her head. "Not in my budget or the Museum's. But I've seen all the photos and been part of getting everything ready. In a way, I've already seen the show."

He turned back to Liam, "When do you leave?"

"Much too early on Tuesday. Kara's going to keep Sadie for me. Wednesday the photos will be hung in the New York gallery. Thursday there's a string of publicity appointments set up by the gallery. Critics asking endless questions. Friday night is the opening. More questions but with champagne and fancy finger food."

"You going to stay a while? See old friends?"

"No. Saturday morning I'm flying to North Carolina to see Tracy. She's feeling neglected and, since I'll already be on the East Coast, I don't have much of an excuse not to visit. She wants me to go through some personal stuff she's been storing for me."

This was the first Kara had heard about that part of his trip. But then there was no reason he should have told her. He'd be gone longer than she expected.

Liam leveraged himself out of the low chair. "I need to go rescue Sadie. She'll be cross about being left at Vince's all day."

In the school parking lot, Johnny opened the passenger door for Kara. "I hope you can come back again."

"I do too."

"Liam looks better than I've ever seen him. You must be good for him."

"Oh no." She realized she was blushing. "It's nothing like that. We just work together." But she wondered whether that was all there was to their relationship. Something more occasionally wandered around the fringes of her thoughts. She glanced over at Liam, hoping he hadn't heard Johnny's remark. Fortunately he was calling Vince to tell him they would be picking Sadie up in a few minutes.

Silhouetting the trees at the edge of Liam's front yard, the Pecos sunset was morphing into a soft peach. Kara sat in one of the upholstered chairs, sipping at the wine she'd brought from the kitchen. Liam was talking to Edgar on the phone, something about the gallery in New York. By the time he came into the living room with his wine, it was almost dark outside. No lingering twilight here. Sadie was stretched out on the floor in front of the fireplace, clearly worn out by her spa day. A bit sulky when they picked her up. She'd eaten her dinner and left the kitchen while they were eating. The dog version of *I'm not ready to forgive you yet.*

Kara leaned her head against the back of the chair. It wouldn't take much for her to fall asleep. All that walking in the cool freshness of Canyon Road. She made herself focus on the four photos on the wall.

"Tell me about your pictures." She took a long sip of wine. When he didn't reply, "I recognize the Eiffel Tower. I bet that was a really difficult shot."

"Hours and hours and lots of wasted film. There's no easy way to get night shots, let alone one with so many surrounding lights. I'm not a fan of digital photography yet, but that shot would have been cheaper in digital."

"Was it part of a job?"

"Not directly. I was in Paris for a job, taking fashion shots. This picture was a challenge I gave myself."

"And the landscapes?"

He didn't answer right away. "The one on the right is in Provence near Roussillon. The one on the left is Brittany, near St. Malo." He reached for his wine and leaned back in his chair.

"The portrait?"

The answer waited, then his voice was so low she could barely make out the words. "My wife."

As though she knew Liam needed rescuing, Sadie chose that moment to stand up and walk toward the door—her ritual request to go outside. Wineglass in hand, Liam opened the door and followed her out, shutting the door behind him. Effectively ending the conversation.

When he didn't return, Kara went to her room to pack. Clearly, she'd stepped over a line.

Even though it was getting cold outside, Liam sat in the rocking chair long after Sadie had finished her nightly rounds, letting the darkness provide a safe hiding place. No question he was being unfairly rude to Kara and, at some point, he would have to apologize. But for the moment, memories were paralyzing him.

He could not explain why, after all these years, he still couldn't talk about Ariane with anyone, not even her family. Whenever he visited Roussillon, they wanted to tell stories of her childhood, reminisce. A healthy kind of grieving. Unlike his grief which, for the first two years, had required large quantities of scotch so he could sleep.

As the date of the gallery opening was closing in, he was less and less sure he'd be able to handle being back in New York. The gallery was six blocks from their apartment on the upper west side. He had no intention of going near there, or anywhere else that could interfere with what little progress he'd made, but they'd lived in the city for eleven years. Hard to avoid familiar scenes and sounds, even smells.

When he finally went inside, the light was off in the guest room.

On the drive back to Flagstaff, Liam was quiet. They stopped in Winslow for a late lunch and pulled into Kara's driveway just before four o'clock. When he didn't say anything, she filled the space. "Thanks for the trip."

"You're welcome." A pause. "Did Edgar talk to you about a last minute meeting Monday morning?"

"Yes, he texted me." She wasn't sure why she needed to be there.

"After the meeting, I'll bring Sadie and her stuff over. Is that okay?"

"Sure." She opened the passenger door.

Liam got out to open the hatchback. "I'll keep Sadie in check if you can grab your suitcase."

Disappointed that her exit was blocked, Sadie jumped into the passenger seat.

Liam chuckled. "She likes to ride shotgun."

Kara pulled the suitcase handle up. "Good to know," and abruptly walked away. Maybe too sharp a response. But if she said anything more, she might have to ask why he had been stonewalling her all day. Ask what she had done wrong. She'd enjoyed the days with him—until the *My wife* response which seemed to erase whatever comfort level they'd achieved. Her question about the portrait was totally reasonable. After all, it was hanging on the living room wall. She couldn't have guessed that he felt— what sounded like—raw pain. His wife was a gorgeous, blonde, with a dazzling smile and eyes that followed whoever looked at the photo.

Such beauty made Kara feel plain. Nowadays, whenever she looked in a mirror, she was confronted with crowsfeet framing her eyes, strands of gray sneaking into her light brown hair—her mother used to tell her it was chestnut because it had natural light streaks, but the lights were definitely fading. Putting in highlights was a lot of trouble and expensive. At least, it was thick, in humidity even wavy. Not much wrong with her figure, but she wasn't 21 anymore. On the other hand, why was she comparing herself to the woman in the photo?

A female habit, nothing to do with Liam. Nothing at all.

She waved briefly as he backed out of her driveway.

Nothing at all to do with Liam.

After the Monday meeting with Edgar, she and Liam put Sadie's bed in Kara's bedroom. When Liam was staying with Kara, Sadie had slept in the guest room. She seemed tentative about this new arrangement. Looking at Liam as if to say *What's going on?*

"It's okay, girl. Only a week." He sighed, "Can't put anything over on her. Someone told me that rescue dogs are often super sensitive to changes, afraid they're going to be left again."

"We'll be fine."

"Sorry I was preoccupied on the drive back."

Preoccupied wasn't the word she would have chosen. "No problem." A small white lie.

"You girls have fun. I'll call after the opening to let you know how it went. I have a return ticket for the 27th."

Then he leaned over and kissed Kara's cheek.

In the hours that followed, neither was sure why he'd done that.

Chapter 10

Liam had agreed to attend the New York opening of the Plateau exhibition by convincing himself he would not go near the crash site. Edgar had booked hotel rooms two blocks from the New Image Gallery, just off Central Park. Fly in, fly out. No reason Liam needed to go anywhere near Union Square.

Yet, on Friday afternoon he found himself standing on Seventeenth Street across from Union Square's Greenmarket, the intersection where his life came apart. Rubbing salt into the wound that had scabbed over but never healed. The outdoor market was always a study in colorful chaos. Ariane loved shopping here for their fruits and vegetables, cheeses and spices. *It feels like a French market. Like home.*

Since she'd quit modeling, she took a taxi to the market on Monday and Friday mornings, caught another taxi home in time to meet her afternoon French classes at a small charter high school within walking distance of their West Side apartment. Two classes: beginning and advanced. *Teaching French verbs keeps me from being homesick.*

To make sure Ariane stayed connected to her family, she and Liam always visited Provence over the Christmas holidays and for a few weeks in the summer. Liam tried to schedule his photo shoots around the trips but, if he was finishing a project, Ariane would go ahead and he'd join her later. She'd been raised in Roussillon, but her modeling career had taken her to Paris—where she met Liam when he was shooting the Paris 2000 Fashion Week layout for *Vogue*.

Whirlwind love.

A month later, she followed him to New York, and they were married in Roussillon that Christmas. Her modeling career transferred quite easily to the States.

This was the second time he'd stood at this intersection. The first time—two days after the accident—he'd vomited in a nearby trashcan, gone home and finished off a bottle of scotch, trying not to see what he kept seeing. Later that year, during the accused driver's trial, the prosecution presented photographs showing what remained of the taxi after the rented U-Haul truck plowed into the back seat where Ariane had been sitting. It was all Liam could do to stay in the courtroom. The next day the driver, who had been high on meth at the moment he drove through the red light, was convicted of two counts of manslaughter while driving under the influence.

Today, Liam was briefly tempted to walk into the nearest bar, order a martini, and hope the alcohol could erase the memories New York had sadistically preserved. But one drink would not be enough, and he'd find himself back on the slippery slope that shadowed the pain without removing it. Another trip to rehab he did not need.

He'd already broken his private promise about visiting the corner where Ariane and the baby died. However, his promise to appear at the gallery at 7 p.m. had to be kept, so he hailed a cab and returned to the hotel. Missing the reception would not be fair to the Museum or Edgar. There would undoubtedly be people at the reception who remembered him and his previous work. And the catastrophe that drove him away from a successful career. As long as they wanted to talk about the photographs—some of his best work if he did say so—he would be okay. It was the personal prying that would make the evening difficult.

Such a tragedy. Where have you been keeping yourself? What are you doing now? Have you remarried?

No one in Pecos or Flagstaff asked those kinds of questions.

When Liam arrived at the gallery, Edgar was waiting inside the front door, leaning on his crutches. Liam smiled, "You clean up good."

Edgar had abandoned his usual Levi's and white shirt for designer denims, a gray sport jacket and gray shirt with a bolo tie. He laughed. "Doesn't happen often. You don't look so bad yourself." Liam had resurrected a black silk suit and lightweight white turtleneck. The upscale clothing and artificial rituals of gallery openings belonged to another time.

The atmosphere in the main hall reminded him of other receptions, other years.

Another Liam.

The Saturday morning headline on *The Times* arts section read *Faces of the Colorado Plateau: A Stunning Collection.* Along with praising Liam's photos, the review included some of Liam's back story, detailing major points in his career and recounting the tragedy that ended it.

But Liam wasn't in town to read the article because he caught the Saturday morning flight to Raleigh. The days in New York had been unsettling; he'd have preferred going straight back to Pecos, but he'd promised his sister he would visit.

After Ariane's funeral in France, Tracy had agreed to put all his photographic gear in storage and dispose of everything else in the New York apartment. Then list it. With a Central Park view and nearly two thousand square feet, it sold the first week. And for the next year, he wandered aimlessly around Europe with a backpack, drinking too much, finally hitting bottom and putting himself in rehab. He wasn't quite a full-blown alcoholic, but close. Once he moved to Pecos, he retrieved his photographic equipment from its New York storage. But now Tracy wanted the personal belongings she hadn't disposed of out of her basement. A project he'd been avoiding for too long.

Not until the Raleigh plane was taking off did he remember he had promised to call Kara after the opening.

To be on the safe side, Kara took Sadie for a walk just after dinner on Friday so she wouldn't miss Liam's call.

But there was no call.

When there was still no call on Saturday morning, she texted Edgar while she was on her break at the Museum. **How was the opening?** Two hours later, he answered, **Fantastic. Pick up a copy of The NY Times at the grocery store.**

She bought the newspaper on the way home and spent the evening reading about Liam's talent and his past, which explained a number of things that had puzzled her.

Tracy's yellow clapboard house was in one of Raleigh's older neighborhoods. She and Seth had bought the house when the boys were still pre-schoolers and, as far as Liam could tell, they hadn't changed its exterior or landscaping all that much. When the taxi stopped at the curb, Tracy was in the front yard, weeding one of the flower beds along the brick path to the front door. She was three years his senior, with a softer version of his lankiness. Her hair was darker and cropped short to cope with the curls that refused to behave whenever she let her hair grow out.

They hugged a long time. "I was afraid you wouldn't come."

He'd been afraid of the same thing. "You look good."

"And you look like you don't eat enough. Do you ever cook for yourself?"

"Still bossy, I see."

"How was the reception?"

"Good, I guess. People saying all the right things whether they meant them or not."

"Still cynical, I see."

"Guilty." He'd missed her, stayed away longer than he should have. "Is Seth home?"

"Yes. Staring at his computer screen. He's teaching an online class this semester and claims it takes more time than if he just went into a classroom and lectured. Fortunately, his other two classes have live students."

He put his arm around her shoulders, "Let's go save him. What's for lunch? I didn't have time for breakfast."

Being with Tracy and Seth felt good, but the ordeal of emptying the storage boxes lined up in the basement confronted him with what had been ripped away. The blackness of that time swallowed him all over again.

Tracy hadn't saved Ariane's clothes, but she had kept the jewelry. "Some of it looks old, maybe family pieces." There were scrapbooks of her modeling career in France and the U.S., as well as records of Liam's photographic career.

Tracy had kept several original paintings Liam had collected over the years; each would bring a high price. There were boxes of file folders: old tax returns, Ariane's lesson plans for her French classes. Boxes of books, his on photography, hers on art and French history.

For three days, he sat in Tracy's basement, weeping over the remnants of his marriage. He wanted no part of these things, but Ariane had two younger sisters who might want the jewelry and her scrapbooks. He told Tracy to sell the paintings and keep the money. Two kids in college did not come cheap. Then trash whatever didn't go to a charity.

He was drained.

Moving to a different state, building a new house, and adopting Sadie didn't mean he'd figured out how to move on. To have a real life. He was almost as broken as the day Ariane and the baby died.

Melissa, they'd planned to name her Melissa Suzanne.

Instead of flying back to Arizona on the 27th, he changed his ticket and flew to Marseille, rented a car, and drove north to deliver the jewelry and photos to Ariane's family. He owed them that.

Tracy promised to call Kara. Sadie would be staying longer than planned.

After reading *The Times'* lavish praise about Liam's photos and the tragic loss of his wife and unborn child, Kara wasn't surprised that he hadn't called about the show's reception. Going back to New York must have been excruciating. She reread the article through tears, understanding his refusal to talk about the portrait in his house, worried what she would say to him when he returned. Not knowing about someone's tragedy was easier than knowing. Could she go back to being *normal* with him?

Then Tracy called.

Momentarily afraid for Liam, "Is everything okay?"

"Yes and no. Liam asked me to tell you he won't be back for a while." When Kara didn't say anything, "He flew to Marseille this afternoon."

"Why?"

"He needed to return some items to Ariane's family. Can you keep Sadie a while longer?"

"How long do you think?"

"He didn't say. He's not in a good place, and it's my fault for asking him to do something about the boxes from their New York apartment. I probably shouldn't have pushed him, but I thought maybe it was time for some sort of closure."

Kara felt her throat tighten. He might not come back or, when he did, he'd be different. And if he didn't come back, Sadie was going to be heartbroken.

"Do you know where he's staying?"

"No, only that he's going to Roussillon, where her family lives."

"Where is that?" Of course, she could Google it.

"Provence. It's a beautiful village, one of the perched villages. Amazing color."

"Thanks for letting me know."

After they said goodbye, Kara found herself crying. For his pain and her own disappointment. As though she knew Liam wasn't coming home yet, Sadie put her head on Kara's knee.

Chapter 11

Kara had lived in Flagstaff just over a year, Michael had been dead two and a half years, and Liam had been gone a month.

Liam's absence felt much longer.

She tried to keep Sadie busy. A walk in the morning, another in late afternoon, and one just before bedtime. Whenever someone came to the front door, Sadie was on alert in case it might be Liam. When it wasn't, her disappointment was palpable.

Liam or no Liam, it was time to hunt down another job.

The photography project had filled in some of the financial cracks, but new cracks would eventually occur. The board at the Museum confirmed the opening date for showing the Colorado Plateau portraits at the Museum: Opening September 14th, the reception on the 15th. That information provided a good excuse to email Liam. She could send a picture of Sadie. Jumpstart some sort of communication. She took several shots of Sadie during one of their morning walks and uploaded them into her laptop. The message needed to be casual, friendly, not nosey. No recriminations about disappearing. After deleting several drafts, she put words in Sadie's mouth.

> *Hey Liam, Sadie here. I'm attaching two pictures Kara took on our walk yesterday. I like the first one; the other one makes me look fat. Kara says that your photos will be hung in the Museum September 12th and that the show will*

open September 14th. Reception the night of September 15th. Tuxedo not required.

Kara says hello. Love, Sadie

No reply.

Sadie didn't notice, but Kara did. It was already June, and she was still taking care of his dog. Paying for Sadie's food, taking her to the vet to have a thorn removed from her right front paw. Didn't all of this dog TLC count for something? Even an LOL would have been acceptable. Liam had been an almost daily part of her life for four months and now, like the other men in her life, was gone.

Getting to be a pattern.

Though her neighborhood always felt quite safe, Kara made sure she took her phone when she and Sadie walked—in case Liam called. As the days were getting longer, Sadie was ready to walk earlier than Kara would have liked, but the air was clear and cool and they pretty much had the small park at the edge of the condominium complex to themselves. Since they were the only ones in the park, Kara let Sadie off the leash. She'd just settled herself at one of the picnic tables when her phone vibrated.

Jeff's picture filled the screen. "Mom?"

The first time she'd heard his voice since his family moved. At 5:42 in the morning. Mother instincts kicked in. "What's wrong?"

"The baby's here. Last night. A boy. Seven pounds, two ounces. Everybody's okay, sort of."

He sounded like he did when he was seven and knew he was in dangerous territory. Trying too hard.

"Ellen?"

"It was a long labor so the doctor finally did a C-section because the baby was in distress. They're both fine, but it's going to require a longer recovery time for Ellie. She'll be in the hospital another week."

Kara had a pretty good idea what his next sentence was going to be.

"If I get you a plane ticket, could you please come? Even when Ellie and the baby get home, I don't know how I'm going to cover everything. School is due to let out."

She couldn't resist. "No paternity leave?"

"I haven't been here long enough. Please Mom." His voice almost cracked.

Parenting and grandparenting didn't seem to come with an off switch.

Probably no chance of a direct apology. She let him wait a minute or two. "I'll have to make some arrangements."

The biggest issue was Sadie. Taking her to Cincinnati was out of the question. She called Edgar. At least Sadie had spent a little time with him in the Museum. His wife, however, was not as willing to help out as Edgar was, so he'd have to take Sadie to his office at the Museum during the day. If things got too tough, Johnny was next in line. Kara called him to explain about Sadie and about Liam being off the radar.

After the phone calls to arrange for Sadie's care, she was ready to give Liam a piece of her mind. And not the nice-lady piece. She understood that he was in a bad place, but her place wasn't in great shape either.

Chet was not as accommodating about her need to go to Cincinnati as Kara had hoped. She would be put on leave without the promise of being able to return to her weekend job if they found someone to replace her. Part-timers, it seemed, didn't have job security.

Fortunately, Kara had all of her bills set up to be paid on line, and Maddy promised to pick up her mail and forward anything else that looked important. She also volunteered to drive Kara to the Phoenix airport.

"Does going to take care of your family seem like a re-run of your move to Flagstaff to take care of the twins?"

The thought had crossed and re-crossed Kara's mind. Parenting always felt that way. Just as soon as you assumed one problem or phase of kid-growing was done and gone, it turned up in a slightly different guise, but was still the same problem. Was she doomed to be at her family's beck and call forever? She craved time for establishing a new life. If kids could go through phases, why couldn't she have a new phase? One that let her experience things and people she'd missed during her earlier phases. Like helping Liam. Like getting back to her art.

"I'm not going there all that willingly. It's just that, if I don't, I may lose even more contact with my grandchildren. Too close can be too close but no closeness isn't a good option either."

"I get it. Keep me posted. What did they name the baby?"

"I forgot to ask."

Her Nana skills were slipping.

When Liam saw Sadie's second email, he knew it was time to break his silence.

> *Liam, FYI my address is changing again. Kara needs to go to Cincinnati to help with the new grandchild and the twins, so Edgar is dog sitting. I miss you. Where are you? Frustrated, Sadie*

> *To: Kara Talmadge, cc Edgar Nunez,*

> *Dear Sadie: Be sure to thank Kara and Edgar for looking after you. I'm back in the States and will be staying in North Carolina for the next few weeks. Don't give up on me. Liam*

Kara didn't see his reply until she was in the Phoenix airport. While she was waiting for her flight, she called Tracy. "Is he staying with you?"

"No. He's not far away though."

"Because?" Kara was tired of Liam's secrecy. Tired of him avoiding her and Sadie.

"Sorry," and Tracy did sound sorry, "but it's his story to tell, not mine." *Not much help.*

"I've had to turn Sadie over to Edgar, at the Museum, but I'm not so sure his wife is going to put up with having a dog underfoot. I'm on my way to help out with my son's family for a few weeks. A small emergency. If you talk to Liam, please tell him that the default arrangement is for Edgar to take her to Pecos to stay with Johnny."

"I will. Thanks so much for looking after her."

They announced the Cincinnati flight. "I have to go."

Tracy called Liam every evening. Her idea, not his. "How was your day?"

His answers ranged from *painful* to *some progress*, without providing details. "How was yours?"

"Kara called, wanting to know where you are, what's going on. She's worried that Edgar's wife, who, it seems, is not a dog person, will evict Sadie before Kara or you can get back. I stonewalled her."

"Thanks for being my gatekeeper."

Tracy was afraid he might revert to living like a hermit. "What would it hurt to tell her where you are? Thank her for running interference with your dog."

"Not ready for that right now."

Not ready to talk to Kara or hear about the dog? He wasn't sure which. Actually not sure about much of anything. His therapy sessions with Dr. Elaine were tough, not designed to make him feel better in the usual sense. And she did not come cheap.

Jeff had the twins with him when he met Kara at the airport in Cincinnati. At their age, six months made so much difference. Not only were they taller, Molly taller than Jared, but they'd shed most of their baby fat.

Both screamed "Nana" as soon as they spotted her and raced to strangle her with their hugs. She had truly missed them.

From Molly: "We have a baby brother. He's to be called Camden Michael."

Camden? Baby names these days were certainly different. At least, Michael got into the mix.

"Have you seen him?"

At the same time, "Oh yes." Two beaming faces.

Jeff was wrestling her suitcase off the carousel. "Just this one?"

"Yes. Thanks."

He looked exhausted. Keeping the twins clean and fed, going to the hospital and, probably, working as much as he could was taking a toll. She knew she was needed. To help convince herself she was glad she had come, she hugged the twins again.

It was almost dark when they got to the house, a two-story white frame, certainly larger than their last house. The front yard beautifully manicured. They must have a gardener—Jeff hated yard work. Once they were inside, Molly grabbed her hand. "Come see our rooms. We each have our own, and Camden will have his own too." In the midst of their excited chatter, she heard Jeff ordering pizza on his cell. Tomorrow, she'd have to go grocery shopping and fix some nutritional dinners. Fill the freezer.

She also needed the keys to Ellen's car and the kids' daily schedule. And of course she'd visit Camden.

Nana was back at the helm.

Her first week in Cincinnati was relatively simple because the twins were in school and Ellen and the baby were in the hospital. She had time to check out the local shopping and found a coffee shop three blocks from the house. After she walked the children to school the fourth morning, she stopped into Ground Rules for coffee. Which is how she met Paul Stewart, who owned the shop and took an interest in all his customers. Especially attractive middle-aged women who were new to the area and not wearing a wedding ring.

Kara ordered a latte and stood at the counter while Paul worked coffee magic.

"I haven't seen you in here before." He had a nice smile, fair hair that was receding, and a tattoo on the inside of his left forearm. Kara was not a fan of tattoos, but this one was amusingly appropriate: an elongated pitcher pouring something dark into a cup. Obviously meant to be coffee.

"I'm helping my son. They have a new baby and two older children, so it's a bit frantic right now."

"When you're not babysitting, where do you live?"

"Arizona, Flagstaff. Do you know where it is?"

"No, but I've heard of it."

He set a white china cup and saucer on the counter. "I'm guessing you'd rather not have your latte in a paper cup."

"You're right." She laid the money on the counter and turned toward the tables. He stepped around the counter and followed her.

When she'd chosen a table, he sat across from her. "Tell me where Flagstaff is."

She did. It was rather nice to talk to an adult. She explained about moving from California to Flagstaff, then turned the conversation toward him. "Have you always lived here?"

"No. Originally, North Dakota. But after I retired from the army, I decided I didn't want to deal with those long winters again."

"But aren't the winters hard here?"

"By California and Arizona standards, yes. But Cincinnati looks pretty good after Fargo."

"I'll take your word for it."

A young woman pushing a stroller entered the shop. He stood up, "Excuse me," and went to the counter. Several more customers came in, all of whom he knew by name. Kara wished they'd had more time to talk, but she needed to go to the hospital. Paul waved as she left. A pleasant start to her busy day.

Ellen and the baby were slated to come home in two days, so Kara spent the afternoon checking things off the shopping list Ellen had given her. Once Ellen and Camden were home, there would be much more to cope with. Not since the twins' arrival had Kara taken care of a newborn. That time there were no other children to complicate the tasks. Pretty soon she would be as exhausted as Jeff. She decided to make meatloaf and stew, a lot of stew, to cover the first week of looking after Camden. Then there were the twin's lunches. She'd forgotten to ask about any special food items for Ellen. She made sure there was plenty of ice cream. Easy dessert.

Nervous about Sadie, Kara emailed Edgar while Jeff was picking Ellen and the baby up at the hospital. *How is she? Maybe more important, how are you?* His answer wasn't reassuring.

> *Twice she's escaped from my office. Once she ended up in the Gift Shop, the other time in the parking lot, headed toward your place. Fortunately, I remembered to have treats. She's definitely not happy about being in Foster Care.*

Midst the chaos of getting Ellen and Camden settled in and keeping the twins from waking him because they wanted to touch him, Kara forgot the Sadie problem. That night, after the family was asleep, she emailed Liam. Not as Sadie, but as her worried self.

> *Sadie is in flight mode. Twice she's escaped from Edgar's office. My best guess is that he's going to get tired of chasing her down and take her to Pecos. Suggestions?*

Short and to the point. She was too tired to try for humor or, for that matter, to be patient. Whatever demons he was fighting weren't helping with Sadie, and not being able to do anything about the situation was not improving Kara's mood.

Chapter 12

Liam's trip to France reopened half-healed wounds and created one or two new ones. Ariane's mother wept over the family jewelry that had belonged to a grandmother, two aunts, a great-great someone else. Because Liam's French was rusty, keeping the lineage sorted wasn't easy. Her sisters, one who still lived in Roussillon and had never married, the other who was married and living in Avignon, ended up fighting over who should get what. *Hell, it was just jewelry.* His earlier trips to her family had soothed the edges of his grief.

Not this time.

To escape, he drove to Brittany. St. Malo had been one of Ariane's favorite places. They had honeymooned there. Unfortunately, the weather was wet and cold—no help for his already sour mood—and so he drove back to Marseille, once again changed his return ticket, and showed up on Tracy's doorstep after only three weeks. In a deep funk. Confused. France usually helped him feel closer to Ariane, to reconnect with the good times. Now he felt like he was twisting in the wind.

Tracy listened to his rambling explanation of why he hadn't stayed longer, then asked a dangerous but long overdue question: "Do you need to get some help? Wait. Let me rephrase that. You need to get some help."

"I'm not drinking, other than the occasional beer or glass of wine."

"There are other kinds of help. I'm thinking of grief therapy. You dodged doing that the last time." She didn't want to minimize what had happened to him, to his life, but she was frustrated by his inability to climb out of the darkness that surrounded him.

"The last time I needed to get dried out more than I needed to deal with—other things. One problem at a time." He knew he was being defensive.

"Agreed. And you've stayed dry. So what else are you doing right now that is more important than feeling better? You pretend that you're okay, but let me tell you this: my brother Liam has never returned, and I miss him." She stopped in case he wanted to argue with her. When he didn't, "I know someone who knows a very good therapist in Asheville. At least look at the possibility."

Tracy was right. Older sisters often were. But mourning Ariane was comfortable. Familiar. He was afraid that once the good as well as the bad memories were gone, Ariane would truly be dead, and he would be a blank sheet of film.

Thus Elaine Archer, Dr. Elaine to her patients, entered the picture. Because her office was in Asheville, he found a motel that would rent by the week and began 2-hour sessions Monday, Wednesday and Friday mornings. On Tuesday and Thursday afternoons, he attended a bereavement support group. The one-on-one sessions with Dr. Elaine weren't nearly as wrenching as having to share his feelings with the other eight people in the bereavement circle. An hour of that was enough to send him back to drinking. Having to directly address what specifically he missed about Ariane and their marriage was agony. And listening to the agony of the others did not lift his spirits.

The questions from Dr. Elaine were painful, just not as public: *Have you tried dating again, what about sex, who in your current life matters to you?*

When, to her last question, he instantly answered *Sadie*, both of them were silent for a few minutes.

"Who's Sadie?"

"My Golden Retriever."

"You've never mentioned having a dog."

"Didn't think it fit into our conversations."

"Where is she now?"

"I left her with the woman who was helping me with the Museum work," he'd detailed that part of his life at their first meeting, "but she's had to go out of town and now I'm not sure where Sadie is. With my boss at the Museum or a friend in Pecos."

"How long since Sadie's been with you?"

"The end of April."

"Do you miss her?"

He smiled, "Yeah."

"Tell me about her."

He did—at length. Her love of ice cubes, her penchant for running away, the way she could read his sadness.

Since her next appointment had cancelled, Dr. Elaine let him continue telling Sadie stories. His usual taut expression softened, he smiled now and then at a specific memory. "She took to Kara right away. I didn't worry about leaving as long as she was with Kara, but now she's reverting to some of her bad habits, like running away."

"You told me last week you didn't think you could ever love another woman. Yet you clearly love Sadie."

"She's a dog, not a woman."

"Noted. But love expressed in any form is a positive sign. You are still capable of giving and accepting love."

He didn't reply.

"Tell me about Kara. Married? Single?"

"Widowed. A few years." It occurred to him he didn't know exactly.

"And? Come on, Liam, help me out here."

"Two grown children. Right now, she's taking care of her newest grandchild in Cincinnati. She works part time in the Museum."

"Was that so hard?"

He shrugged and checked his watch. "It's past time."

"Don't think this discussion is over. Next time I want you to tell me more about Kara. And I need to read what you're recording about our sessions and your feelings."

Busted. He'd have to get something down on paper in the next two days. He hadn't been able to write what was swirling around in his head. Probing the wound didn't seem to be helping. No wonder he'd spent so many years ignoring it as much as possible.

When Tracy called the next morning, she told him Edgar was, at that moment, delivering Sadie to Johnny. "He said it was either that or divorce."

"Did he sound mad?"

"No. He sounded rather nice. You're lucky to have people willing to pick up after you."

"I know." Tracy was one of them.

He needed to touch base with Edgar. Dog sitting was not in his job description. And asking about the September show at the Museum would be prudent. He had no idea how long he'd be in North Carolina once his sessions with Dr. Elaine were over. It might be too easy to crawl into his cocoon again. Wasting all of Dr. Elaine's work—and his. She wanted him to look at the future. Create his future. Something beyond playing tennis and walking Sadie. Blazing a new trail in photography? Problematic. He didn't see himself setting up shop, taking on clients as he had before. A profitable career, which was still bankrolling most of his day-to-day expenses. How does a person create a new life? Late forties, not much of a human network, though his professional reputation seemed to be intact—if he could believe the reviews from New York. No nuclear family requiring his attention. At least Kara had children even though she wasn't always happy about some of the ways they still made demands on her. Maybe not having demands on him was part of the problem.

His life would be different if the baby had lived, if he had that connection. If. The doctors had tried to save her. Melissa lived one day longer than her mother but was too fragile to confront the world on her own. He'd never held her. A father without being a father.

Dr. Elaine started their next session with, "Tell me about Kara."

He sighed. "She's originally from California. Her son was working in Flagstaff, so she followed him and his family. Then he moved to Cincinnati."

He recounted their first meeting, Sadie escaping the Museum, then Kara filling in for Edgar on the photo project.

"You haven't told me what she's like. Attractive?"

It took him a few seconds to answer. "Yes, more wholesome than glamorous. Light brown/blonde hair, I guess you'd say medium length. Doesn't use much makeup. Mostly casual clothes, but part of that is Arizona. I don't think I've ever seen her wear heels." Ariane had worn heels even with denims. "She's easy to talk to. Definitely a grown up." No drama

"You like her?"

"Yes." An easy answer.

"Are you attracted to her? As in *attracted*."

A harder answer. His response was a shrug. Sometimes there was an undercurrent. Perhaps that's why he'd kissed her cheek. But attraction might be overstating what he felt. The concept of anything more than a brief affair scared the hell out of him. Committing himself to another woman just opened up the threat of being hurt, of loss. There was no way he could survive two losses. Better not to risk a deep connection.

"Okay, for contrast, tell me about a woman you don't like."

"Ariane's sisters." He'd never figured out how Ariane could be so sensible and lovable and her sisters such pains. All drama. The whole jewelry issue was typical.

And then, "When's the last time you had sex?"

He was close to speechless. A question too far. "A year or so."

"Who was the woman?"

A thirty something blonde he'd met at an art exhibit in Albuquerque. They'd had a late dinner and one thing led to another. She'd been the one who seduced him. He stayed over, then went back to Pecos to take care of Sadie. End of story.

"In other words, just sex."

He nodded.

"Tell me about your marriage."

When he didn't answer, "How long?"

"Eleven years." Why was she asking this? She knew the answer.

"Describe Ariane. Since she was a fashion model, I'm guessing she was tall and thin. Graceful, if you subtract the runway walk."

"A natural blonde, she tanned easily. French through and through. Sexy, funny. Didn't have to watch her weight like some models do. A superb cook." He took a breath. "She loved me." He'd been so blessed. Some men never have someone like her. Eleven years was too little, but better than not having those years. *Maybe he was making progress.*

"A sense of humor?"

"Yes, but humor is tied to language so English double entendres were lost on her." She took his teasing well; she loved to surprise him with unexpected gifts. Make him his favorite foods. She took food seriously. Was impatient with the quality of American bread and was always looking for the perfect boulangerie which, even in New York, was difficult to find. If she were living in Pecos, she'd probably be baking her own bread. If she were living in Pecos, she might not like the isolation. Even small French villages were social places, conversations in cafes, knowing everyone's business. A community. His memories wandered the vibrant streets of Roussillon. Narrow streets, cafes with views of the red ochre landscape.

"Where have you gone, Liam?" Dr. Elaine was tapping her pen on the notebook she always had in front of her.

"Sorry."

"What were you thinking?"

"That she probably wouldn't like Pecos. Too isolated and even though people are friendly and helpful, the town doesn't have the same energy. The same excited noisiness. Sometimes, when we were in Provence with her family, I'd finally take a walk, just to find silence. I grew up with space around me. My dad had a small ranch in Southwestern Colorado. He wasn't a full-time rancher. He was also a teacher."

"Where do you see yourself in five years?"

"No idea."

"In three months."

"The photos will be at the Museum in mid-September, so I need to show up for the opening."

"That's one night."

"True. I can't predict any farther." As with relationships, not having goals prevented failing to meet the goals.

"Can't or won't?"

"Don't want to."

She stood up. "Okay, now we're getting somewhere. On Wednesday, tell me why. Session's over."

This was one of those days he felt bruised all over after she finished with him. And when Tracy's name showed up on his cell phone the next morning, he let it go to voice mail. He could explain how film was made, how a camera was put together, but explaining his fears and feelings was nearly impossible.

He needed to touch base with Edgar and Johnny. Would it be totally stupid to put the phone to Sadie's ear, so she could be reassured by his voice?

After his *mea culpa* conversation with Edgar, he called Johnny. "How is she?"

"A bit droopy but otherwise okay. I took her out to your place yesterday after school and let her sniff everything. Her nose should be exhausted. But I think it helped."

"I mailed you a check this morning. If I need to send more, let me know." He needed to reimburse Kara too.

"No problem. My cats, however, will probably scratch your eyes out the next time you show up. I'm going to have to put them on valium. Not because Sadie's done anything to them, just because she's a dog."

Liam laughed. "Would it help if I talked to her on the phone?"

"Let's see." A door opening, then, "Okay, I'm holding the cell phone by her ear."

"Hey girl." An instant sharp bark. More barking, the friendly kind. "I miss you too, girl."

More barking.

Liam was laughing when Johnny came back on the line. "How much longer are you going to be?"

"Not sure. Most days I'm ready to cut and run, but my sister would hunt me down and drag me back. Tough lady."

"Run from what?"

"Some overdo therapy. Trying to get my head on straighter than it's been. To answer your question, maybe mid-August. Is that okay?"

"Maria and I aren't going anywhere."

"Thanks for stepping in." When he hung up, Liam made a note to find a top of the line tennis racquet as a thank you. Johnny's was looking a little down at the heels. New Mexico teachers' salaries were not all that great. He needed to think of something for Edgar too.

True to her word, Dr. Elaine started the session with "Why not?"

The answer had kept Liam awake a good portion of the night. "Because rebuilding my life comes with risks I don't want to revisit. I can still work when and how I want to, where I want to. I don't need to be out on the front lines proving I'm photographer of the year any more, but I'll probably never stop being a photographer. I made good money and invested it well; the Manhattan apartment was a small goldmine." Listening to his own answer made him realize how empty his life sounded.

"So when I send you my bill, the check won't bounce."

"Hope not. I might have to get a new bank."

"Now, about your personal life."

"I can't face the prospect of losing people I care about. Can't go there again. My insides are scoured out. Nothing left."

"Fear then?"

"Okay."

"Were you a good husband?"

God, the woman could slice and dice his brain in a single sentence.

"A good lover." Let her deal with that answer.

"Eleven years with a French wife, you'd have to be or she'd have gone home. I said husband."

"I think so. A little preoccupied with my work sometimes. Ariane expected attention. But she had her modeling career for the first ten years. She started teaching French when we were trying to get pregnant. She knew her figure would change but that was okay. She wanted a child."

"Did you?"

"Yes."

"Because she did or because you did?"

"Because I did."

She leaned back in her chair, her eyes boring into what passed for his soul. "Again, where do you want to be in one or two years? Alone? Working? And don't tell me you're not alone because you have Sadie."

"I don't know."

She straightened in her chair. "A life is a terrible thing to waste. You don't have to remarry or have children, but you have to have people in your life somewhere, a reason for getting up in the morning. Not just to walk the dog. Come back with better answers on Friday."

He was close to telling her to go to hell but that wouldn't solve anything. How could she expect him to fix himself in two days? He hadn't managed that in seven years.

Kara had forgotten what it felt like to be sleep deprived. Not just wakeful because of worry, but jarred out of deep and necessary sleep by Camden's middle of the night yowl. An impatient child. The twins had been much less trouble during the night, but then they'd slept in a two-fer bassinet. Automatic companionship. She tried to get to Camden before the entire house was awake. Because Ellen was nursing him, she pumped milk for nighttime feedings, leaving that task to Kara. The theory was that Ellen would recover from the C-section faster if she could sleep through the night. She nursed him when he woke in the morning, allowing Kara to sleep in. Jeff got breakfast for the twins and took them to the summer playgroup. Fortunately, Jeff wasn't working weekends.

The one bright spot in her day was her morning walk to Ground Rules. A bit of conversation with other customers or Paul—and then back to Jeff's. Four weeks into her visit, Paul invited her to have lunch with him the following Sunday. "It's the only day we're closed."

A date? Kara was pleased, albeit taken aback by the invitation and a little nervous. She enjoyed talking to him. A quiet anchor in the midst of busy days. Accepting his invitation was easy. If, as Beth had suggested, she didn't need to be alone forever, Paul might be a good person to spend time with. To practice what was left of her dating skills. He was probably in his late fifties, twice divorced, one son, one grandson in college.

He suggested meeting at twelve thirty, at Jimmy's Café, just down the street from the coffee shop. "I go to Mass at eleven."

Two divorces and he still went to Mass. Interesting.

She didn't tell the family where she was going and neither Jeff nor Ellen asked. The young Talmadge household had many other things going on— play dates, shopping trips, naps, laundry. And more laundry.

Sunday was hot and muggy. Kara missed the dry heat and the cool nights of Flagstaff. Cincinnati had neither. She wore a sleeveless blouse and cotton slacks. Sandals. After all, it was lunch, not dinner. Paul wore chinos and a plaid shirt. Dressier than what he wore in the coffee shop. He was waiting on the bench outside the café.

"You look cool and comfortable."

"Not too easy with this humidity. California doesn't have much humidity; Southern Arizona does have a summer monsoon, but this 24/7 stickiness is new."

"Humidity is a fact of life in the Midwest. Balanced by ice storms and fifty mile an hour winds in winter. Let's go in, Sergio is saving us a table by the window." He held the door for her.

The restaurant was bustling with families. Kara ordered breakfast, French toast stuffed with cream cheese and scrambled eggs. Paul decided on a hamburger and fries. "I ate breakfast before Mass."

"I had coffee and oatmeal hours ago. My son loves oatmeal; that's always on the stove Sunday mornings. The twins hate it, so they have cold cereal. The baby doesn't get a choice, just milk."

"How old is the baby now?"

"Almost six weeks."

"Does he sleep through the night? I remember being truly relieved when my son finally slept six hours straight."

"Not often enough. But some nights he might sleep five hours. Fortunately, once he's been changed and fed, he goes right back to sleep. I envy him that ability."

"What about the other two?"

"They could sleep through almost anything. I've started giving them art lessons."

"You're an artist?"

"Was, sort of. I can certainly give them the fundamentals. Molly loves it and may actually have a bit of talent. Jared, on the other hand, only wants to know how to draw dinosaurs and robots. Not exactly in my skill set."

"Why did you give up art?"

"Two kids and a husband who worked sixty hour weeks. Most of the household chores were mine. And when my daughter entered middle school, I began working in his law office."

"You should go back to being an artist."

She was getting closer to actually doing that.

"I'm thinking of asking the art store in Flagstaff if I can offer art classes for children. I tried to get a job in the store when I first moved to Arizona, but they didn't have an opening. Since art is seldom taught in elementary schools these days, my idea might work. I'm practicing on the twins."

"I never had any creative urges, except for putting cinnamon designs on cappuccino foam."

Their orders came and they concentrated on eating. Then lingered over coffee, discussing TV shows and books. A relaxing afternoon. He walked her back to Jeff's but didn't come in.

Chapter 13

Johnny texted Kara that Liam's phone call to Sadie had perked her up for a while, but she was back to sulking. Kara wished Liam would call her too. She could, of course, have texted or emailed him, but she didn't want to assume he wanted to hear from her. The second week of September the Museum would be hanging the Colorado Plateau portraits, and she was beginning to fear he might not show up.

Though she and Jeff were on slightly better terms and she'd had quality time with her grandchildren, being in her own space was looking better and better. Camden was thriving, and Ellen had been cleared to drive. Less need for Nana. Her excuse for leaving Cincinnati came when Maddy phoned, "Did you know your daughter is staying at your place?"

"No." A flicker of fear crawled along her spine. Another family fire to put out.

"When I stopped for this week's mail, I went inside like I always do, and there she was, sitting on the couch, watching TV."

"How did she get in?"

"My first question. She said you gave her a key the last time she was here."
More that Lindsay hadn't given it back.

"Thank you for the heads up."

Time to leave Cincinnati.

Jeff made her plane reservation and paid for the return ticket to Phoenix. "I really appreciate you coming to help. I hope you can forgive me for leaving you in Flag." The *good* son. Apology appreciated. Nevertheless,

Kara wasn't sure she was ready to forgive him just yet, especially since coming to Cincinnati had cost her the job at the Museum. At least she'd had time with her grandchildren.

She did, however, need to tell Paul she was leaving. She walked to the coffee shop, waiting at a vacant table until he was free.

"I'm flying home tomorrow."

"Isn't this rather sudden?"

"A friend called to tell me that my daughter is at my place instead of at her place in Hawaii. I need to find out what's going on. She's eight months pregnant and probably shouldn't have been flying."

"Why not call and ask?"

"She's an expert at stonewalling me, especially when I can't look her in the eye." She sighed. "Besides, I need to find another job."

"I'll miss you coming into the shop."

And in a way she'd miss going to the shop, but she really needed to get back to what passed for her own life. Whatever that was going to be. Picking up after her children kept getting in the way.

She wished Liam would get in touch because she wasn't sure what to do about Sadie. Would she have to drive to Pecos or would Johnny keep her?

Kara took the shuttle from Sky Harbor Airport to Flagstaff. She didn't want to warn Lindsay she was coming back or ask Maddy to pick her up. The shuttle dropped her off at the bus station, and she called a cab. She really needed to know how to use Uber. It was nearly seven o'clock when she unlocked the front door and pulled her suitcase into the hallway. She smelled fried chicken.

Lindsay was standing at the kitchen counter, eating a chicken leg, a KFC barrel and a large container of coleslaw in front of her.

"Looks like there's enough for two or three."

Lindsay looked up, totally surprised. Score one for Mom. The baby bump had been replaced by the baby bulge and was barely covered by the tee shirt she was wearing. Her black leggings were stretched to the max. Lindsay obviously hadn't shopped for clothes to accommodate her expanding middle.

"What are you doing here?"

"What are you doing here?"

Lindsay leaned against the counter, still holding the chicken leg. "I suppose your friend ratted me out."

"Yes."

Though the conversational ball was squarely in Lindsay's court, she made no move to pick it up. And Kara wasn't willing to help. "I'm going to take a shower. Save me some chicken."

Discouraged, Liam was contemplating canceling his appointments with Dr. Elaine. Whatever counseling was supposed to do wasn't working or not working enough. He didn't know what he'd expected—perhaps instantly returning to the man he'd been before Ariane's death. Wishful thinking fueled by Tracy's eagerness to help. What he knew was that there was no quick fix, or any fix at all. He was permanently damaged.

On Wednesday, Dr. Elaine was late. Twenty minutes into what should have been his appointment, she hurried through the door, more disheveled than he'd ever seen her. Sunglasses pushed onto the top of her head, carrying a Starbuck's coffee cup. Vente.

"Sorry." She dropped into the chair opposite his. "I hate to admit it, but I was in the middle of an argument with my teenage son. I always thought a psychology degree would smooth all paths, including my own." She drew a deep breath and took a sip of the coffee. "Did you and Ariane ever argue?"

Not a direction he anticipated.

When he didn't answer. "Did you?"

"Sometimes."

"What about?"

"Usually our schedules. Mine mostly, especially if I had a big project. I would be obsessed."

"How did you get past your disagreements?"

"Talked them through; and soon. We didn't let problems accumulate. But the morning—" he stopped.

"What morning?"

"The morning of the accident. She asked me to go to the Greenmarket with her. We were having company that weekend, and she knew there'd be a lot to carry. I suggested she wait until later that afternoon, but she was worried that the best of everything would be picked over by then. She was in her seventh month and more emotional than typical. Impatient. I should have—"

And there was the sticking point. He should have gone with her. If he'd been with her, the scenario would undoubtedly have been different. He felt his heart begin to race, the panic that washed over him was like the panic that had haunted him for the first years he was alone. It hadn't happened like this for a while.

"I never—I never had the opportunity to make it right. And I wasn't with her. She and the baby were alone—all alone in that damned taxi!" He gripped the chair arms, forcing back tears. He did not want to cry.

Dr. Elaine set her coffee down and leaned forward, no note pad this time. "Are you okay?"

"I'm sweating."

She reached over to take his hand. "I think we're onto something important."

He moved his hand away.

For the rest of the hour, neither of them said a word. Liam couldn't, his throat had closed against revealing what he remembered and regretted so much. She gave him the space to process the memory.

And to confront the self-imposed guilt.

Tracy was the only person he'd ever told about the guilt. She'd flown to New York the night Ariane died, handled as many of the gruesome details as she could, leaving him huddled in the bedroom. Too stunned to move. Whenever Tracy asked him something, he could barely whisper *yes* or *no*.

Tracy contacted Ariane's family, made arrangements for the two caskets to be flown to Roussillon for the funeral. Liam hadn't cared about the funeral, didn't want to attend, but Tracy and Seth went with him, made sure he didn't wander off. Ariane's family needed him to be there even if he didn't think he needed to. He didn't go to the wake. Couldn't deal with the whole open casket thing.

It seemed as though the entire village attended, as well as a few of Ariane's Paris friends. Liam looked like death, his eyes were sunken, and he'd lost weight; his suit hung on him. Immediately after the funeral, Seth flew home because he was teaching a summer class, but Tracy stayed so a local lawyer could do the preliminary paperwork giving Tracy Liam's power of attorney. "You'll need it to sell the apartment for me. I can't go back."

"It wasn't your fault." She knew she was spitting into the wind.
"Indirectly it was."
They didn't see one another for two years.

At the next therapy appointment, Liam was still reeling from having revisited his guilt. Miraculously he was sober, though not heading to the nearest bar had been difficult. Dr. Elaine came loaded for bear. She'd had two days to readjust her strategy. Instead of getting him to talk, "Just listen. Don't interrupt. Listen. When I'm done, you can tell me to go to hell or take what I'm about to say to heart.

"You are wasting your life. You're a good-looking, talented, caring man. You have gifts to give, but you don't think you have anyone to give them to. So you give little, except maybe to your dog, and take little. Even when it's offered. You've created an intentional loneliness. You're punishing yourself and indirectly punishing those who know you and care about you.

"You lost your wife and baby. Will that be the sum total of your life? If so, you might wish to find a very high bridge and get your life over with." She stopped. When he didn't protest, she stood up. "I think I've failed to provide the help you're looking for. You want a magic answer. I don't have that kind of answer. You need to get on with your life. Stop feeling sorry for yourself. You're not the only one to lose your family."

Liam stayed in his chair, not noticing when she left the office. He didn't have an answer either. But something in Dr. Elaine's diatribe hit home. He was pretty sure he didn't want to die. His weeks in Ashville had actually made a small difference in the way the world looked.

Lindsay Talmadge had never been given to introspection. Deep diving into her innermost thoughts wasn't comfortable and had rarely proved helpful. Normally, when she had a problem she couldn't unravel, she'd go surfing. The fresh air and water and exercise scrubbed away whatever uncertainties were snapping at her. Once back on the beach, she could again manage her life. Well, usually. This baby sloshing around in her belly was preventing her from surfing. She was afraid of falling, of hurting the baby. So she was stuck on land and for the time being, dealing with Max being in another hemisphere. She missed him—big time.

A month ago, a surfing friend offered him a job in Perth, setting up a training program for surfers wanting to compete internationally. Max would design and oversee the training while his friend would publicize and manage the events that would, hopefully, draw surfers from around the world. And so he went. If the idea took off, they might be surfing entrepreneurs instead of surfing bums. He was used to going when and where the surfing was good. But now that he was going to be a father, she hoped he would rein in his wanderlust.

"Babe, I can't pass up this opportunity. Do you want to come?"

"I can't surf. Shouldn't be flying that far and I have a job that's going to pay my hospital bills."

OMG. She'd become practical. When had that happened?

He left her the keys to his house—the girls she'd been living with had already rented her room to someone else—flew to Singapore, then to Perth. Two weeks later, Lindsay decided to visit her mother. Those two weeks rattling around in his house by herself made even Flagstaff appealing.

She was pretty sure she was going to regret turning up at her mother's. Questions would be asked. Her mother always asked questions. Lindsay rarely shared her life with her family. But right now she was alone, the baby was due soon, and she wasn't sure she could do this alone. She really, really hated admitting she couldn't do something.

Max's texts were all about how great the surfing was, how beautiful Australia was, how well the program was doing and, sometimes, how much he missed her. He was handsome and charismatic—obsessed with surfing. And now he was half a world away, and she was watching daytime TV at her mother's.

This was not what she'd hoped for.

Kara took a longer shower than she usually did. Washed her hair. Even used the hair dryer. She needed to approach her daughter carefully. Staying calm was the key. Kara was in no mood to get trapped into more Nana duties right now. The weeks in Cincinnati had been sufficient.

Having grandchildren was a pleasure—most people would say a blessing—nevertheless, taking care of them long term was not on her agenda, or what passed for her agenda. Just because she didn't have a husband to take care of didn't mean she wanted other people, especially little people, to take care of. She'd gone along with the move to Flagstaff because, well, because she couldn't afford California and perhaps because she hadn't quite recovered from Michael's death. Currently, she was as recovered as she would ever be. It was time to be herself.

There needed to be boundaries.

Lindsay was asleep on the sectional when Kara came downstairs a little after eight. Probably just as well. She ate three pieces of chicken and finished off the coleslaw, found a vending machine package of Oreos that hadn't been opened, and took it to her room. Time to begin the book she'd been carrying around for weeks. Lindsay's crisis would wait until morning.

With no more appointments in Asheville, Liam drove to Tracy's. Not to stay, just to spend a night and explain that he'd been cut loose. Dr. Elaine was undoubtedly correct. He was the only one who could fix himself. He wasn't sure the sessions had helped, but revisiting New York City may have. He was no longer afraid of it. A very small step.

Johnny left a phone message for Kara:

> *Two days ago, I had to put Sadie in the Doggie Sleepover, even though she hates it. I don't know where Liam is or whether you're still in Cincinnati. Anyhow, she did a runner last night. The vet scoured Pecos but no luck. Best guess, she might head for Liam's cabin. Maria and I are in Texas for a family funeral and the vet has a business to run. What are the odds that you might have time to drive to the cabin? She might be trying to get home. Liam keeps a spare key under the mat at the shed door.*

Chapter 14

Kara listened to Johnny's message while she was making coffee the next morning. Her first thought was *Damn, I just got home.* Her second, *We've got to find her.*

She tried Liam's cell. It went to voicemail.

Then Tracy's. More voicemail.

Next, she went online and pulled up "Vets in Pecos" to remind herself of the name of the place where Sadie had been staying. Margaret, the receptionist, was eager to explain. "She got out around two o'clock yesterday. We've posted her information and picture on our website and notified Animal Control, in case they pick her up. Thankfully she has a chip."

Kara printed out a Google satellite map so she could study the route from Pecos to Liam's cabin. She had no idea how long it would take a dog to walk that distance—if that was where she was headed. The fictional Lassie had found her way home but could Sadie? She'd moved around a lot in the last year.

Clearly, this was not a Scarlett O'Hara situation. Kara couldn't put Sadie's flight off until tomorrow. So much for sorting out Lindsay and looking for a job. She knocked on Lindsay's door, then opened it a crack. Her daughter was curled—as much as the baby allowed—under the sheet. "Lindsay."

Not even a twitch. She'd always been good at playing possum.

Firmer and louder, "Lindsay, come on, wake up. We're going to New Mexico. Now."

New Mexico got her attention. She sat up, all young and rumpled, still tan even though she hadn't been in the water recently. "Why?"

"Liam's dog is missing, and no one else is available to go looking. Hippity hop," a phrase that worked with the twins but probably wasn't appropriate for a twenty-six year old. "Get in the shower and pack a few things. We might be there a day or two."

"Where's Liam?"

"I'll explain in the car." Which probably needed gas. She opened the suitcase she hadn't unpacked last night, decided repacking would take more brainpower than she had right now, closed it, and put it in the car, dirty laundry and all. If she remembered correctly, Liam had a washer and dryer.

By the time Lindsay was ready, there was gas in the car, and the GPS was set for Liam's cabin. Two hours had already elapsed. They'd do well to get to Liam's by evening because they'd have to stop and eat someplace, and Lindsay was probably going to need to pee more often than she used to. All they had in the car were four energy bars and two bottles of water.

Kara had no idea how to find a dog. When they lived in Torrance, Jeff's beagle had accidentally been left behind after a day at the beach. The kids had been frantic but, when they returned to the beach an hour later, George was patiently sitting on the sidewalk near where they'd been parked, as if to say, *I knew you'd be back.*

Sadie's situation was more complicated. Hopefully, there was a leash in the cabin and dog treats. But then what? Driving all the roads between the cabin and Pecos? Maybe Sadie wouldn't stick to the roads. Kara wasn't prepared to go cross-country. She didn't have boots and, without established roads and signs, she would be easily lost. Then someone would be out looking for her.

First they had to get to Pecos.

Half an hour into the drive, Lindsay was finally alert enough to remember her earlier question: "So where's Liam? Why can't he take care of his own dog?"

Why indeed. Whatever was going on with Liam remained a puzzle. "He left the Tuesday before the gallery show in New York. The day after the opening, he went to North Carolina to see his sister since he was already on the East Coast. He was supposed to be back here the following Wednesday."

"But it's been a couple of months, right?"

"Three and counting. In between, I went to Cincinnati, he went to France and now he's back in North Carolina. I think being in New York upset him. I could probably get the answer from his sister, but I'm not sure he'd appreciate my prying into his personal life."

"Since he's dumped his dog on you, you have some right to pry."

"I offered to keep her. He didn't dump her."

Lindsay frowned. "You don't stand up for yourself. People ask things of you and, even when they inconvenience you or you really don't want to do whatever it is, you do it anyway. You always let Dad and Jeff and me impose on you. Case in point, Cincinnati."

Amazingly perceptive---for Lindsay. Another case in point. "So if I throw you out of my guest room, you'll understand it's because you're inconveniencing me?"

Lindsay actually laughed, "I guess."

"So why are you inconveniencing me?" More important to find out what was going on with Lindsay than trying to explain Liam.

"Max went to Australia."

"And?"

"I'm sort of at loose ends" A pause. "He may not come back any time soon. It's a great opportunity to set up a surfing camp that will train people to enter international competitions."

"Are you going there?"

"Not until the baby's born. I'm not supposed to fly now. We didn't actually talk about the specifics. It all happened so fast. He just said *I'm leaving Friday.*"

And so Lindsay was going to have the baby in Flagstaff. Kara needed to get her head around that fact.

"Where have you been living?"

"In his place—our place." She looked at her watch. "Since I'm awake now, why don't you let me drive for a while? At some point, I'm going to get sleepy. I'm always sleepy lately."

Kara pulled over at the next rest stop, and they changed seats. She'd probably gotten as much information as she was going to get right now. And besides, she was the one who was sleepy. She was still on Cincinnati time.

Liam turned the rental car in at the Raleigh Airport and bought a Michael Connelly paperback at the airport newsstand. His ticket to

Phoenix included a three-hour layover in St. Louis. There seemed no way to go cross-country without one or two stops. He was flying into Phoenix because he needed to retrieve his SUV, which was still parked at Edgar's. The bills for rental cars, both in the states and France, were substantial. He needed his own wheels.

Because he'd been off everyone's radar since the night of the New York opening, he definitely needed to check in with the Museum to find out when the next round of photos was scheduled, and he owed Kara an apology. In the midst of his self-imposed anguish, he would suddenly think of her—want to tell her something like he did when they were working at the Museum. Talk about Sadie, share part of his day. He was surprised every time it happened.

Not until he checked his voicemail during the shuttle ride to Flagstaff did he catch Johnny's message about Sadie. He punched return but it went to voicemail. So he tried Edgar.

"I'm glad you called. We need to talk about the next shooting schedule. Where are you?"

"In the airport shuttle, somewhere on the Black Canyon Highway. Has my friend Johnny Salas called you about Sadie?"

"No, why?"

"She's once again on the loose, somewhere around Pecos."

"Sorry, I can't help you with that. Should I pick you up at the bus station?"

"If it isn't too much trouble. I need to get my car and head to Pecos as soon as I can." He was worried about Sadie but no sense dumping his concern on Edgar, who had already tried to help with the dog. Tracy was right. A lot of people were picking up after him. "I'm due in Flag at 4:30."

During the drive east, the only conversation Kara and Lindsay had was about Liam. The baby and Max didn't make another appearance. Outside of Grants, when Lindsay woke from her second nap, she saw a McDonald's billboard, "I'd love an ice cream sundae."

Kara insisted Lindsay also order a fish sandwich. "You need protein. Maybe I'll get one too and a salad; you can have part of it. This'll have to count as dinner."

Strangely enough, Lindsay didn't argue but, while they ate, she continued giving Kara the third degree about Liam.

"So what's the mystery?"

"I don't know the details. His pregnant wife—her name was Ariane—died in some sort of accident in New York, seven or eight years ago. After the New York show, *The New York Times* did an article on Liam's work. Her death coincides with his giving up his photographic career. According to the article, he was a major figure in studio photography. He did mostly fashion and portrait work. Some urban photography. I suspect he made a lot of money." She finished the last of her coffee. "Come on. Let's get back on the road." It was after six. "I don't want to be looking for the cabin in the dark, even with the GPS."

Once back in the car, "So he just disappeared for all those years?"

"At least as far as his career is concerned."

"And ended up in the back of beyond in a cabin with a dog. It would make a great Hallmark movie." Lindsay fastened her seat belt, making sure it was below the baby and started the car. "How much longer?"

"Maybe two hours."

She pulled expertly onto the Interstate. Michael had taught her well.

"Do you know what she looked like? His wife."

"Blonde, quite beautiful."

"Where'd you see a picture?"

"It's on the wall in his living room."

"You've been to the cabin?"

"Before the gallery opening. In April." No sense hiding that part. Let Lindsay think what she wanted. Nothing had happened. However, the longer Liam was gone, maybe gone for good, the more Kara wished *something more* had happened.

Thank goodness for the GPS. Kara could never have figured out the turns in the forest. "There's the row of mailboxes. We're close."

Thunder rumbled overhead. Lightning briefly illuminating the road, then more thunder. "It sounds like it means business." Kara leaned toward the windshield, "There's the cabin." More lightning.

"That's a house, not a cabin."

"My thought exactly. Let's get inside before the rain hits."

They grabbed purses and suitcases and made it to the porch just as fat, hard raindrops splattered on the porch roof.

Kara unlocked the door, flipping the light switch. All the lamps turned on at once. Comforting light to counteract the storm.

Lindsay walked across to the windows. "This is amazing. A front row seat on the storm. How come you have a key to his house?"

And there was the suspicious Lindsay.

"When he left Sadie with me, he gave me the key. Just in case."

"Really." Not quite sarcastic.

"Don't go there. I'll look for a flashlight. Maybe Sadie's out back, though if she's come this far, I'd expect her to be on the front porch. It's her favorite spot."

Even though she found a flashlight, Kara delayed her search of the backyard until the rain stopped. But there was no Sadie, just plenty of mud on her tennis shoes. She left them on the back porch. They'd have to be scrubbed.

Lindsay was lying on the sectional. "Please tell me there's a shower somewhere."

Kara pointed. "The towels are in the closet in the hall. Are you okay?"

"Sure, just tired. I feel like we're still driving. I can hear the road noise." She was pulling her top over her head as she walked toward the bathroom.

Kara looked into Liam's room. There were no sheets on the bed. She didn't feel right about sleeping in his bed but was too tired to explore that reluctance. She went to look for fresh sheets so the bed would be ready when Lindsay got out of the shower. The bed in the guest room had fresh sheets. She'd prefer sleeping where she had when she visited in the spring.

By nine-thirty both of them were in bed. No way to look for the dog tonight. Hopefully it would be drier tomorrow.

Lindsay was up and dressed before Kara, making coffee in Liam's Keurig. "I'm ready to go. Sadie's been on her own a long time. I hope she's okay."

Here was the caring Lindsay that Kara hadn't seen in a while. Sadie's plight had touched her daughter, who had always loved animals.

"Will you call the vet's office while I'm getting dressed to see if there's any news? The number's in my phone. And would you please plug my phone into the charger in the car? I forgot to do that overnight."

The vet's office had nothing new to report.

With each passing hour, Kara's fear for Sadie increased. Liam couldn't afford to lose someone else he loved.

They began their search in East Pecos, up and down the streets, stopping now and then to call Sadie's name. Kara finally turned the GPS off. Their random driving was making the robot voice crazy. It was almost screaming *Recalculate*.

By noon, they'd covered a large portion of the open space between East Pecos and Pecos proper. Before they went looking for lunch, they decided to drive back to the cabin to see whether Sadie had shown up.

No Sadie.

They drove until it was too dark to see, stopped for gas and groceries in Pecos, and returned to the cabin.

Still no Sadie. They checked with the male voice on night duty at the vet's, then heated up Stouffers' beef stew. Exhausted and worried, they again were in bed early.

Kara was sound asleep when her cell chimed the next morning. "This is Margaret at the vet's. Animal Control just called. Someone in East Pecos found Sadie alongside a road just before dawn. She's been hit by a car." Kara was instantly awake.

"Is it serious?"

"The clerk that called us didn't know. Animal Control took her to the Santa Fe Emergency Animal Clinic. It's a couple of blocks west of St. Francis Drive. They handle after hours care for small animals. I have their address and phone number."

"Let me get something to write on. Could you also give me the number for Animal Control? We need to know who found her so we can thank them."

Once again she was rousting Lindsay out of bed. At least this time they knew where Sadie was. In fifteen minutes, they were in the car, Lindsay in the driver's seat. They turned the GPS back on and entered the clinic's address. Kara was both relieved and afraid, already rehearsing how she'd tell Liam—if she could make contact with him—that Sadie was injured. Because she couldn't seem to quiet her thoughts, she was glad Lindsay was with her. Her daughter was good with animals, had often taken better care of George than Jeff had.

The drive to Santa Fe seemed longer than it really was. Kara's stomach was growling; dinner had been a long time ago. When they pulled into the clinic's parking lot, it was just after eight o'clock. "Come on Mom, let's go."

Uneasy about what they might face inside, Kara got out of the car slowly. She knew she was being a coward. What if Sadie died or would have to be put down? How would all of them handle that? Especially Liam.

Lindsay was holding the clinic door open, "Hurry up."

Chapter 15

The small lobby was empty, a landline phone on the desk ringing persistently. After it recorded the name and number of the caller and clicked off, an eerie quiet surrounded them. Impatient, Lindsay peered down a hall that led off the lobby. "Should I go look for someone?"

"Maybe we should stay here for a bit. Someone probably heard the phone."

As though Kara hadn't spoken, "I'll go look." Lindsay turned into the hall and disappeared from Kara's sight. Left on her own, a collection of worst-case scenarios raced into her head. Worst of all: Sadie dying and Liam's distress, even anger that she left Sadie with Edgar and Johnny. If Sadie did recover, how long would that take, where would she stay? Could they take her to Flag?

The vet's phone call had jump-started her morning. She definitely needed coffee, but there were no vending machines in sight.

Because her nerves were running rampant, Kara looked around for a restroom. Nothing like anxiety to make her have to pee. Maybe it was located down the hall Lindsay had followed. Preparing to explore, she slipped her purse onto her shoulder just as Lindsay was framed in the hallway, smiling. "She's going to be okay."

Momentarily forgetting about finding the restroom, Kara dropped into the nearest chair, giving in to grateful tears. "Oh thank God." What was it that made her cry when news was good? She wiped at the tears with her hands, "Is there a restroom someplace?"

"I'll show you. I've already used it." She led the way down the hall and pointed to the right. "I'll go back to the lobby. The vet was not thrilled that I was back here."

As soon as they had been briefed on Sadie's condition, Kara called Liam's cell and was shocked when he actually answered. "Kara? Where are you? Have you found Sadie?"

She took a deep, steadying breath to keep the tears from resurfacing, "Lindsay and I are at the Emergency Animal Clinic in Santa Fe. It's the only place that accepts injured animals after regular hours."

"She's hurt?" His distress reached through the phone and grabbed her heart.

"A car hit her last night and left her on the side of the road. Someone in East Pecos found her and Animal Control brought her here." She paused, "Luckily she's micro-chipped."

"How is she? Have you seen her?"

"Not yet, but the vet explained that her left hind leg is broken in two places. They operated to put pins in and she's still sleeping off the anesthetic. He figures she's bruised too; they did an MRI and everything else looks good."

"That's a relief. Thank you so much for making the trip to look for her. Are you staying at my cabin?"

"Yes, until they release her. Where are you? At your sister's?"

"At Edgar's. I didn't listen to Johnny's voicemail until I landed in Phoenix. I came to pick up my car, and Edgar and I have been going over the next portrait schedule. I'm planning to head for Pecos early tomorrow so I'll be able to take care of her. Can you stay until I get there?"

"Yes. If they release her today, we'll take her to your place." How she and Lindsay would manage that she had no idea.

"Do you have the phone number for the clinic? I need to give them my credit card information." He was pretty sure emergency surgery was going to be expensive.

She read the clinic number off a business card she found on the reception counter. "The vet is Dr. Theo Mendez."

As it turned out, Dr. Mendez wanted to keep Sadie another night. "Just to be sure."

Too emotionally exhausted to do anything else, Kara and Lindsay stopped in Pecos to buy groceries and more ice cream——Lindsay had gone through what they'd bought yesterday—and went back to the cabin. Naps were high on the agenda. Since Liam would arrive tomorrow, Kara needed to change the sheets on his bed again and move Lindsay into the guest room with her. On second thought, she might prefer the couch. Lindsay and the baby took up a lot of space.

As she drifted into her nap, she was aware of a soft excitement that had nothing to do with Sadie being safe.

Liam left Edgar's just after ten. It was strange that Sadie wasn't in the car with him. He rarely took a road trip without her. At least she was safe and would heal. But he blamed himself for neglecting her for so long. Her accident was indirectly his fault. Up to now, his actions had only hurt himself and, sometimes, Tracy. This time they hurt Sadie and inconvenienced Kara, as well as Edgar and Johnny. Too many years of his life frittered away feeling sorry for himself. Few human connections. Standing still or, worse, walking backward.

As he drove east on I-40, he enjoyed the panorama of afternoon clouds piling up along the horizon, promising a much-needed rainstorm. It felt good to be home.

The drive between Pecos and Flagstaff usually took Liam five or six hours. This time, because he was intent on getting to Sadie, he made the trip in a little over four hours. Luckily, no one had clocked his speed. When he reached Albuquerque, he texted Kara.

Is Sadie still at the clinic?

She must have been watching for his message. An immediate **Yes.**

I'll be there in an hour.

All morning, Sadie had been watching for something or someone. Instinctively alert. The intern whose job it was to keep injured pets company was sitting on the floor beside the padded basket Sadie had been moved into. Her injured leg was in a lightweight fiberglass cast to keep the pins in place while she healed. Earlier that afternoon, the vet had helped her stand, letting her experiment with walking on her three good legs. Not too successful yet, but she didn't seem to be in pain today so the medication was working. Unlike most dogs, she didn't object to the pain pill being smushed into her food.

Liam walked into the lobby just before three o'clock. Sadie heard his voice before she saw him and made a valiant effort to get up by herself—but she was only half way out of the basket when he entered the room.

"Hey, girl," he knelt down and held her head between his hands, "It's okay. Lie down. I'm back." He kissed the top of her head. "Sorry to be gone so long."

She yipped softly, and Liam wanted to believe it meant forgiveness. He was sitting cross-legged on the floor with her when Kara and Lindsay arrived a few minutes later. Kara joined him on the floor, reaching over to stroke Sadie's back. "She's glad to see you. She can't take her eyes off you."

He almost laughed. "I have that effect on women." More seriously, "Thanks for everything you've done." He moved his hand to cover hers. Letting it rest there. "How are you?"

"Better now that she's okay. And you're here." He was thinner than when he left, new threads of gray in his hair, which as usual needed a trim.

Reluctantly she moved her hand. His eyes searched hers for a brief second, then shifted back to Sadie. "I'm glad I'm here." To Lindsay, "You've changed since I saw you last."

"Too much ice cream will do that. Since you two have things in hand, I'm going to the restroom."

After she was gone, "When's the baby due?"

"Mid-September. Though first ones take their time." Too late, she regretted saying it. His baby never had that option.

They sat silently until Lindsay returned, "Dr. Mendez will be here in a minute. This time he didn't give me trouble for being in the back hallway."

Kara stood up. "How do you want to get her home?"

Liam looked over at Lindsay, "Can you still get behind the wheel?" He added a grin.

"Barely."

"Why don't you take your mother's car back to my place, then Kara can sit in the back of my car with Sadie."

"In that case, I'll take off now. Should I stop for pizza? I'm starving."

"Sure." He pulled his wallet from his back pocket and handed her several bills. Maybe a Caesar salad too. How are you on ice cream?"

"Good. We loaded up last night. It seems to be a late pregnancy issue for me." She headed for the lobby.

Liam watched her leave. "She's not as edgy as the last time at your place."

"For whatever reason, being pregnant seems to have mellowed her. The father has taken off for Australia to arrange some sort of training program for surfers. I don't have any details."

"Is he coming back?"

"Hopefully. Long ago I learned not to interrogate my daughter. The gates come down quickly. I just play it by ear."

"Mr. Kincaid?" Dr. Mendez interrupted them. Kara thought he looked even wearier than yesterday. Too much night duty at the clinic.

Liam shook his hand. "Thank you for helping Sadie."

At the mention of her name, Sadie moved to stand, then thought better of it.

"She's been a good patient. Though she can let you know when she's ticked off."

"I know that all too well. What do we need to do for her now?"

It took another fifteen minutes of lists, a prescription, and setting up an appointment with the vet in Pecos to check on Sadie's progress in a few days. "We're only the emergency stop. Your vet can contact us if there are questions. Did you bring her bed so we can transfer her? She hasn't mastered walking with the cast."

"We didn't think of that. Sorry."

"No worry. Use the one she's in and bring it back tomorrow."

Sadie weighed close to sixty pounds, so getting her into the car required Liam, Dr. Mendez and Kara. Once they got to Liam's, he and Kara would have to cope on their own because Lindsay shouldn't be doing any heavy lifting. Kara slid into the back seat next to Sadie's borrowed basket and, as soon as the car was in motion, Sadie dozed off.

Getting her out of the car and into the house took time. Negotiating the distance from the car to the porch steps required Rube Goldberg creativity. Liam brought his wheelbarrow alongside the car, then slid the basket into it. So far so good. However, at the bottom of the porch steps, the whole operation suddenly struck Kara as funny. "Thank goodness no one is watching us."

Joining her mother's laughter, Lindsay pulled out her phone, "I'm putting this on Instagram," and clicked several times. When she showed Liam the pictures, he rolled his eyes. "We do look inept. If Sadie could laugh, she would."

Liam took hold of the wheelbarrow handles. "Let's leave her in the wheelbarrow. I'll pull and you push. That's probably easier than juggling her and the basket."

Lindsay held up her phone again.

Maneuvering the wheelbarrow onto the porch was probably easier on Sadie than on Liam and Kara. The most delicate part was transferring her from the clinic's basket to her own bed, but Sadie didn't complain.

Lindsay turned off the video, "Enough entertainment. I'm starving."

"Did you get pizza?"

"Two large ones." Lindsay was already sliding slices onto plates.

Liam picked up the borrowed basket and took it to the front porch while Kara curled herself into the couch, studying Sadie. She suddenly felt lighter, so relieved that Sadie was where she belonged.

And Liam was back.

They left Sadie's bed in living room since, at some point, she would need to go outside. Kara and Lindsay turned in before ten. Wearing a t-shirt and tennis shorts, Liam decided to sleep on the couch. "I want to keep an eye on her."

Kara fell asleep the instant her head touched the pillow but woke a couple hours later, her heart pounding, dreaming that Sadie was still lying in the road in pouring rain. Careful not to disturb Lindsay, she slipped on her robe and went into the living room to make sure Sadie was okay. Liam was awake, sitting forward with his elbows on his knees, watching the dog.

He looked up, "Can't sleep?"

"I was dreaming she was still lying in the road. You okay?"

He nodded and made room for her next to him. "Too wound up."

They sat side-by-side, staring at the sleeping dog. "I don't know what I'd do if she'd died." Liam's voice wavered a little.

"I know." And she did know. Uncertain about asking, Kara asked anyway. "Where have you been? Your sister mentioned France."

Hesitantly, "I was in France for a few weeks."

"And then?"

"Well—usually going there has helped," he assumed Tracy had told Kara why he went to France, "but not this time." Silence. "Once I returned, Tracy guilted me into getting therapy. Grief therapy."

More silence.

"My sister can be a formidable person."

"Did it help? The therapy." *Help* seemed such an empty word for something as enormous as Liam's grief. In grieving for Michael, Kara had learned, was still learning, that the politically correct platitudes—*it'll get better, when a door closes, etc. etc.*—were useless and deeply annoying.

"The jury is out." Liam shifted his position and put an arm across her shoulders.

When Lindsay got up to raid the refrigerator a little after 3 a.m., she found them sitting on the couch, sound asleep. Liam's arm around her mother. There was something oddly sweet about the scene. She was tempted to go back for her phone, then decided they might not want to know she'd seen them asleep against each other.

Liam woke as soon as Sadie began moving around, trying to get out of the basket. He glanced at Kara, asleep against him, eased his arm from around her shoulders, and went in search of an old beach towel. When he came back, Kara was yawning. "Does she need to go out?"

"Yeah. There's a stack of old newspapers in the utility room. Can you grab some and spread them on the front porch? I'm going to try using the towel as a kind of sling under her hindquarters. Hopefully, I can get her as far as the papers. I'll wash off the porch later."

Sadie cooperated until they got to the newspapers, then looked at Liam as if to say *Really?*

"Sorry girl. This is the best I can do now. Tomorrow we'll improve the system."

If dogs were given to sighing, Sadie did, and then proceeded to empty her very full bladder on copies of *The New Mexican*.

Lindsay emerged a little after ten, groggy and hungry, "Is there any pizza left?"

Knowing she shouldn't take the bait, Kara gave her a mother-look, "For breakfast?"

"I get to eat what I want. Once I'm nursing, I suppose I'll have to go off spicy stuff. Are we going back to your place today?"

"I haven't thought that far. Why?"

"I have a doctor's appointment for a sonogram tomorrow morning. My doctor in Hilo made the appointment for me before I left. I got a text reminder a few minutes ago."

Kara would have been quite happy to stay with Liam and Sadie but, because Lindsay was close to delivering, missing the appointment wasn't wise. She found Liam on the front porch, building a temporary ramp with scraps of plywood, gradually sloping it into the front yard. "With this, I should be able to slide the basket by myself. I suspect Sadie's going to figure out how to move better in a day or two."

"It seems my daughter neglected to tell me she has a doctor's appointment tomorrow. We're going to have to drive back today."

Liam looked disappointed. "Is she going to stay with you after the baby comes?"

"Don't know."

He smiled—she wished he would smile more often. "Ah yes, no interrogation. I understand. Would you mind dropping the clinic's basket off on your way? I don't want to leave Sadie alone right now. I promised Edgar to be back in Flag the second week in September. That's when the portraits will be hung. Hopefully Sadie will be more mobile."

"I'm afraid my spare room is occupied. Do you have some place to stay?"

"The Museum's letting me use the cabin again. The new shooting schedule starts the first week of October. Has Edgar talked to you about helping me? Would you like to finish the project?"

More than you know.

"Yes I would, and no he hasn't. But I keep leaving town."

He smiled. "I'm glad you want to. I'll tell him when I talk to him." They stood looking at each other, neither quite sure what should be said next.

They heard the wheels of Lindsay's suitcase in the hall and moved farther apart. "I'm packed."

"Okay, let me get my things. I never unpacked." And was still carrying around dirty laundry.

Lindsay stopped beside Sadie, "Imagine that I'm petting you, Sadie. I don't bend over too well right now." She blew her a kiss and went out to Kara's car.

Kara made a quick stop in the bathroom, retrieved her suitcase and purse, and came back to pet Sadie. "Be good. Get better." When she stood up, Liam was beside her.

"Do you have everything you need? Money for gas?"

"Credit card money. We'll fill up in Santa Fe when I return the dog basket. Do you have enough food for you and Sadie so you don't have to leave her alone today?"

"If I hit a snag, I'll call the grocery in town. They'll deliver." He pulled her into a hug and kissed her cheek. "Safe journey. Let me know when you get home."

All the way to Flagstaff, she felt his arms around her, remembered the kiss and replayed their middle of the night conversation. For just a moment, he'd let down the wall that protected his life with Ariane.

Lindsay slept until Kara pulled into the condo's driveway.

Chapter 16

To LSK70@gmail.com: 9:20 p.m., 8/24: We got home just before seven o'clock. Lindsay slept most of the way. How's Sadie? K.

To Kara1@gmail.com: 10:06 p.m., 8/24: Sadie is trying to get herself up. Clearly she doesn't like my attempts to help her. Ate her dinner but promptly spit out the pill. She's feeling better, I guess. I'm attaching a picture of her almost standing. L.

She looks a little drunk. I drove Lindsay to her doctor's appointment today. This is the first time she's met the doctor who'll deliver the baby. Everything seems to be on schedule. The sonogram doesn't show that the baby has turned yet, but the doctor isn't concerned. The target for delivery is September 13th. I'm not counting on it. We need to shop for a few basics. My daughter-in-law is sending a box of clothes that Camden has already outgrown. Fortunately, a lot of newborn clothes are not color specific. K.

Progress. Sadie's hobbling on three legs. The squatting is hilarious but my help is not graciously received. Is the baby a girl or boy? It sounds like the baby and the Museum opening *are going to double up. We've had thunderstorms the last two days. It's quiet around here without you and Lindsay. L*

It's a girl. I stopped by to see Maddy and thank her for keeping an eye on my place. I took her an azalea for the counter in the lobby. She gave me the names of some thrift shops that might have bassinets and a changing table. I think we can get by otherwise. I went looking for Edgar but he was meeting with one of the new photo subjects. K

Took Sadie into Pecos for her check up. Getting her in and out of the car wasn't easy, but we pulled it off, sort of. X-rays show that she's healing faster than either vet expected, so she has a new, lighter cast to help her put some weight on that leg. No more pain pills were prescribed. I didn't mention she's been avoiding them anyway. How is Lindsay?

Give Sadie a kiss for me. I'm so glad she's doing well. Lindsay is getting bigger and crankier because she's uncomfortable. She spends most of her time on the sectional watching TV. When do you think you and Sadie will be coming to Flagstaff?

Maybe the 11ᵗʰ. She has another appointment on the 9ᵗʰ. While I'm at the Museum, could you take care of her at your place?

Absolutely. Might improve Lindsay's mood.

L indsay had never before felt so miserable. The baby was pushing on her bladder, bouncing around like she was tired of being trapped in a womb. Bending over was almost impossible. Flip-flops were the only shoes that went on easily, and putting on any article of clothing took an incredible amount of time.

Nothing was easy these days. Things had always been easy for Lindsay. She'd always been determined to chart her own path. Going to college in Hawaii had been a way of evading parental oversight and having great surfing. Admittedly, life hadn't been terrible in the Talmadge household.

Just bland. She wanted to be somewhere more exotic. Meet exotic people. And surf.

Enter Max. A mixture of native Hawaiian and Filipino. An accomplished surfer, four years older than she. He'd dropped out of college in his junior year to take his surfing talents around the world, returning to Hilo when the money ran out.

And now Max was half a world away, with no timetable for his return. If she joined him in Australia, she'd have to apply to the district for leave. But so far he wasn't suggesting she and the baby come anytime soon. Accommodations were scare. He was living in a makeshift dorm. Until the baby was old enough to fly, Lindsay was stuck in Flagstaff. At least, her mother could help take care of the baby. To that end, she was experimenting with being the "good" daughter. No ocean, no Max, and the return of parental oversight.

The Sadie episode had been a welcome diversion. But now she was back to watching too much television, taking very short walks, and going to the bathroom every hour. By the time all of this was over, she'd probably look like a novice on her surfboard. She was pretty sure her mother wasn't going to come to Hilo to help her out. Jeff had used up most of her mother's interest in taking care of grandchildren.

"Are you ready to go?" Kara was holding her purse and car keys. "Where's your backpack?"

"In the kitchen maybe." Lindsay pushed herself forward and slowly hefted herself off the sectional. So much effort just to stand up, though sitting down wasn't any easier. What had made her think having this kid was a good idea?

Kara disappeared and returned with Lindsay's small red backpack. She could sympathize with her daughter's discomfort. She remembered that the end of each pregnancy was torture. The passenger seat was pushed as far back as possible but getting in was still a challenge. Lindsay finally fastened the seat belt and sighed. "Can we ask the doctor to induce labor or something? Surely this kid's ready to come out and is just being stubborn."

Kara started the car. "You'll need to ask Dr. Angelo." They had put Lindsay's small suitcase in the trunk of the car three days ago, just in case they weren't at home when her water broke or contractions began. Neither of them could concentrate on much of anything else.

Fortunately, Liam and Sadie would return in two days. Something to look forward to.

His last email had included a picture of Sadie more or less standing, looking pretty much like she always had. *She's healing but is still wary about putting her full weight on that leg. At least she can take care of business without my help. I am seriously grateful for that. I'll text you when we get in.*

And with my luck, thought Kara, Lindsay will go into labor the instant they arrive.

Not only was Lindsay's life on hold, so was Kara's.

Waiting for the new grandchild.

Waiting for Liam and Sadie and the second stage of portraits.

Waiting for other people's lives to get sorted so she could sort her own.

To deal with her frustration, she worked up her courage and revisited The Art Depot with a proposal for a beginning art class for elementary school children and one for adults. For the children, two afternoons after school. For the adults, Saturday afternoons for two hours. She had no idea what to charge or how much of a percentage to offer the art store.

The Art Depot was on a corner with glass display windows on either side of the door and another facing a side street. Maybe she could design a flyer advertising the classes and display it in one of the windows. If the store was interested.

Besides the male clerk, the only other person in the store was at the checkout counter, buying a few tubes of oil paint, long handled brushes, and a large canvas. Kara browsed in the watercolor section—her classes would be in watercolor—to see if there were supplies that beginning students could purchase without investing too much money right away.

"May I help you with something?" The clerk was standing alongside her.

"I have an appointment with Mrs. Osca. I'm Kara Talmadge."

"Okay," he pointed toward the black lacquer door at the rear of the store. "She's in her office. Just knock."

Kara felt her stomach tighten. She wished she could, just once, go into a new situation without being nervous. Would Edith remember that she'd inquired about working in the store? She knocked softly and an equally soft voice told her to come in.

Edith Osca was fortyish, wearing denim slacks and a bright red tunic.

Her long blonde hair was pulled in at the neck with a red scarf that matched her tunic.

"Hi, Kara. Nice to see you again. Please have a seat."

Kara relaxed. This interview might not be so bad after all.

Two hours later, she had good news. She wished Liam were in town so she could talk to him in person. Missing someone was a new experience for Kara. Michael had rarely been out of town—no missing required. He hated being away for more than one or two days at a time. He didn't like staying in hotels, usually finding ways to get Adam to go to legal conferences in his place. Routines and familiar places were preferred. Always had been. When he had agreed to fly to Flagstaff over Thanksgiving to see the newborn twins, Kara was shocked and grateful. He had, however, refused to go to Hawaii until Lindsay's graduation though Kara had flown over with Lindsay at the beginning of her freshman year and stayed a week, sightseeing and shopping, doing what she wanted to do when she wanted to do it That time she had not, admittedly, missed Michael.

The missing that followed his death was different. There would be no moment of reconciliation, only memories.

She definitely missed Liam.

He texted her as soon as he and Sadie had settled into the Museum's cabin: **Can you come by tonight?**

Yes.

She'd been holding her breath all day, praying Lindsay would not go into labor.

Lindsay was lying on the couch, ear buds connected to her iPad. To get her daughter's attention, Kara put herself in her line of vision, forcing her to pull the buds out.

"My cell is on if you need me. I'm going to see Liam and Sadie. They're at the cabin."

"Kiss Sadie for me." The ear buds went back in.

When she parked beside the cabin, Liam was—as usual—sitting on the porch steps, Sadie stretched out beside him. They seemed to be drawn to porch steps.

As Kara opened the car door, Sadie leveraged herself up and, with a rather lopsided gait, met Kara halfway. Liam let the dog get to her first, waiting till Sadie had been given the appropriate amount of petting, before he put his arms around Kara. "Hi."

A bit surprised, in a very good way, her arms quite naturally circled him. "Hi back." Hugging a man you just might be interested in was different from other kinds of hugging. She and Liam stayed close a fraction longer than the usual welcome home hug, then reluctantly separated. Liam smiled. "Thanks for coming over."

"You're welcome." An inane response. Her reaction to being so close to him was interfering with her ability to string intelligent words together.

On cue, Sadie pushed against Kara's leg, looking for more attention. Dogs were good at filling in the awkward places between their humans.

Kara rubbed Sadie's head. "I know, I know. More petting."

"She's good at working the sympathy issue. Come inside where it's cooler."

Kara stayed longer than she intended. She'd told Lindsay to call if there were contractions or if her water broke. Liam filled her in on the next round of photos, gave her a copy of Edgar's tentative shooting schedule, then ordered Chinese food from the Oriental Palace.

Over dinner, she gave him her guess on when the baby was due, explained as best she could about the whole Max situation, and outlined her interview at the art store. "So they'll offer the kids' class for two months. Starting in January."

"Are you pleased?"

"Yes and a bit nervous. I'll need enough students to make it worth Edith's time but not too many that I can't give them the attention they need." They had agreed that seven or eight would be manageable. They still had to decide what to charge because the advertising would be going out soon.

"More rice?" Liam held out the carton.

"I'm stuffed. You finish it." She looked at her watch, nearly nine o'clock. "I should check on Lindsay before she turns in." She scrolled through favorites and found the number. It took several rings for Lindsay to answer.

"Were you asleep? Everything all right?" Kara listened. "Okay." And hit the red button.

"All quiet?"

"So far. She was in the bathroom. She spends a lot of time there."

They went into the small living room with cups of the tea that came with their meals. Sadie lay down in front of the open screen door.

"When does the cast come off?"

"Maybe next week. I have the name of a local vet since I probably won't have time to get to Pecos before the reception."

"And hanging takes place when?"

"Tomorrow morning. Can you come?"

"I have an appointment at the art store at ten o'clock. But I'll drop by afterward." *Unless Lindsay goes into labor.* Everything was contingent on Lindsay.

When Kara got home, the guest room door was closed, giving her time to savor the evening. Being with Liam felt—right. Like she was where she belonged. The problem was—did he feel the same way? The specter of the glamorous French wife loomed large. Dying at thirty-five undoubtedly kept Ariane's beauty frozen in Liam's memory. Kara had never been glamorous. There was no way she could compete with a dead French model. It was quite possible there would never be room for someone else in Liam's life.

The Museum reception for the Colorado Plateau photos began at 5 p.m. Friday night. Wine and hors-d'oeuvres. Liam wore a lightweight tan sport jacket and black slacks instead of the tux he'd worn at the New York opening. A tux seemed a bit too much for Flagstaff. The Museum's public relations office sent one of their interns to take publicity photos of the event and make sure each of the artists was photographed alongside their portrait. Several were wearing their ceremonial outfits.

The turnout was encouraging.

Though Liam was kept busy talking to the attendees, he was simultaneously waiting for Kara to arrive. Edgar's opening remarks explained that there would be more photographs sometime next year, and then he turned the podium over to Liam for questions. Liam had planned to introduce Kara and thank her for her help, but by six o'clock, she still hadn't arrived. Liam finished answering questions half an hour later and walked into the hallway to check his cell phone. It wasn't like Kara to be late.

He found two texts. One at 5:32: **I'm not going to make it. Lindsay's water broke** and a second message at 6:30. **We're at the Medical Center. This kid is in a hurry.**

He answered briefly: **I'll come by as soon as I can.**

He didn't leave the Museum until a little after eleven.

Chapter 17

At the Medical Center, Liam found Kara on a bench outside Lindsay's room—leaning against the wall, her eyes closed. Carefully, he sat beside her and reached for her hand.

"Oh," she turned, "I didn't know you were here."

"That's because your eyes were closed."

She found the energy to smile, "True. I couldn't keep them open another second."

"Is everything okay? Is the baby here?"

"Yes. Both are fine. They're cleaning the baby up, weighing her, taking her footprints, all the things they do. Sorting Lindsay out too. She came through brilliantly."

Kara was remembering the look of relief on Lindsay's face when Kara walked into the delivery room. The baby was coming in a hurry. Lindsay grimacing while trying to pant her way through the contractions. When the contractions eased for a moment, "Mom, stay—with-me," and then the next contraction took over. It had been a long time since Lindsay had asked Kara for help.

Two hours later, Baby Girl Talmadge came into the world, wailing. If Kara remembered correctly, Lindsay had arrived the same way. Thoroughly upset at finding herself in a strange environment. Jeff, on the other hand, had needed encouragement to cry. A quiet child from the beginning.

Four grandchildren.

Somehow, Kara hadn't minded being a grandmother when the twins were born, but then she was not quite forty-five and Michael was still alive. In today's world, barely middle-aged. After all, some women were having their first child at forty, but turning fifty in a few months put a different spin on the Nana label. She didn't feel old—**was not old.**

She stole a side-glance at Liam—still holding her hand. She'd always liked having Michael hold her hand. Missed the comfort of that simple gesture. Liam's hand was wrapped around hers, surrounding more than holding. Nicer than holding.

She leaned back and again closed her eyes.

Liam had never actually seen a newborn up close and personal. When Melissa was on her way, he'd wondered what it was going to be like to look into the face of the tiny human he'd help create. Tonight, riding in the Medical Center elevator, he fought back the memory. At this point in his life, there would probably never be a child with his DNA. Dr. Elaine had cautioned him not to ruminate or create what-if scenarios. *You can't heal if you keep pulling the scab off. Instead, think of something to be grateful for—now.*

Something to replace the painful memories.

He looked down at Kara's hand within his and let himself be grateful he'd come to the hospital. She'd had a long, stressful evening, being strong for a daughter who was not always appreciative. Kara seemed so self-sufficient. Capable. Willing to help with Sadie and also help her son's family even after they decamped to another city. Liam had been no better, leaving her to cope with Sadie.

Kara didn't wake up when the door to Lindsay's room opened and a nurse signaled they could come in. Liam leaned over and lightly kissed Kara's lips.

For just a second she kissed him back; then, fully awake, she straightened, ending the kiss.

"You can go in now," he nodded toward the nurse. "I'll wait here."

Kara stood, "Lindsay won't mind."

"I'll give you a few minutes first."

Lindsay was sitting up in bed, holding the baby, who had just had her first try at nursing. Lindsay's expression was a cross between exhaustion and amazement. Kara had never seen her daughter look prettier. "How did the feeding go?"

"Okay, I guess. We're both sorta new at this. She fell asleep after a few minutes."

"May I hold her?"

Lindsay carefully transferred the tiny bundle. Kara looked approvingly at her second granddaughter, whose coloring had definitely come from Max—rosy-tan skin and a hint there might eventually be black curls. "Did you choose a name?"

"Malia. It's a fairly common name in Hawaii. And she looks Hawaiian. Isn't that neat?" She held out her arms. "Gimme."

"Do you mind if Liam comes in for a moment?"

"No problem. What about the reception?"

"It's over."

Kara held the door open and motioned to Liam.

Hesitantly, he walked to the side of Lindsay's bed. "Congratulations." He couldn't think of anything else to say. Definitely not a situation he had encountered very often

"Do you want to hold her? Her name's Malia." For the second time, Lindsay held out her daughter.

"Maybe I should just look. I've never—"

"Go ahead. She's sleeping."

He let Lindsay place the baby on his outstretched hands. Kara came alongside. "Put her in the crook of your arm." She helped. "Now hold her against your chest." He followed instructions, mesmerized by this brand new person—impossibly tiny. Dr. Elaine was wandering around in his head, telling him this was a moment for gratitude instead of sorrow or envy. He was definitely grateful there was no panic attack.

After a few minutes, he returned Malia to Lindsay. "She's beautiful." Her eyes locked on the baby, "How was the reception?"

"Good. Bigger crowd than we expected. Thanks for letting me hold Malia." To Kara, "I'll be outside."

When Kara walked out of the Medical Center, Liam was in the parking lot leaning on her car. "I'm driving you home. You're tired. We can collect your car tomorrow."

Kara considered protesting but knew she was emotionally and physically wiped out. She was glad he had waited.

"Is there anything in your car that you need?"

She shook her head. "We left so quickly I barely remembered my purse. I was only focused on Lindsay."

"My car's over there," he pointed.

Kara was pretty sure she'd never before been rescued this way. Others always seemed to need her to rescue them.

He left her at her front door. "Sadie's been on her own all evening. She needs to get outside." He gently put his arms around her and, for the second time tonight, kissed her. "Call me when you're ready to pick up your car."

Enjoying the sensations set off by his kiss, she could only nod, and then she was alone in front of her open door. In the months Liam had been gone, something in him seemed to have changed. Opened up.

But she was too exhausted to deal with anything other than getting into bed.

Alerted by Kara's phone call, Liam and Sadie were on her doorstep just after nine, Liam carrying two cups of coffee and a sack with two croissants. Sadie had a pink *Baby Girl* balloon tied to her collar. "She is not thrilled that the balloon is following her around, but she wanted to come see you. Did you sleep?"

"Surprisingly, yes." Though the kiss, not the baby, had initially interfered with falling asleep. He didn't need to know that. "I called Jeff and my parents this morning and then checked with Lindsay. The hospital isn't going to release her until tomorrow morning. She sounds tired but gave me a list of things she wants me to bring to the hospital. A day without her make up is a bad day; it seems she forgot to pack that."

Liam untied the balloon and retied it to the handle on the pantry door while Kara warmed the croissants and poured orange juice for both of them. This felt like the days when he was staying with her during the water heater repair. Back then, however, he hadn't kissed her the way he did last night.

"Sadie's getting her cast off later this morning. The vet took another x-ray yesterday, and she's good to go. She'll be a much happier dog."

"What about the rest of your day?"

"Edgar and I are reviewing comments people left on the cards we handed out at the reception. And he wants to look at the website with an eye to including any rave reviews that will promote the next show. That should take most of the afternoon. Since Lindsay is staying in the hospital one more night, how about I take you to dinner tonight?"

She finished her croissant and wiped her buttery fingers on a napkin. The invitation didn't sound like the usual *Let's grab a bite when we finish work* dinner. The words *take you* suggested something more. A date?

"I'd love to." She was a little short of breath. "I probably won't spend too much time with Lindsay. She wanted me with her yesterday, but today could be a different story."

"I'll check in later."

He dropped her at the Medical Center and headed for the vet's office.

Kara stayed with Lindsay and Malia until just after noon, then treated herself to a manicure. Not something she did with any regularity, but tonight she wanted to look her best. There just might be another kiss on the menu.

The rest of the afternoon was spent changing the sheets in Lindsay's room and readying the bassinet for its new occupant. When she was done, she took a short nap on the sectional, then filled the bathtub, and soaked in some of Lindsay's bubble bath. A day to indulge herself.

Liam called as he was leaving the Museum. "I made a reservation for seven o'clock; is that okay?"

"Should be. How's Sadie?"

"Euphoric. She thinks she's a puppy."

As soon as Liam ended his call, her parents, anxious to meet their new great granddaughter, phoned to say they'd made train reservations from San Jose to Flagstaff and would be arriving in three days, automatically assuming there would be room for them. When Kara was living in Torrance, there was always enough room. These days, her parents rarely traveled, especially since her father hated flying. The train trip would take them nearly twenty-four hours, so they'd reserved a sleeping compartment. Could she meet them at the train station Tuesday morning at 6 a.m.?

When Liam picked her up, her head was still whirling with the logistics of soon having four family members in her condo. He was in chinos and a short-sleeved cotton shirt—what passed for dinner attire in the Southwest. Kara was glad she'd chosen a sleeveless cotton dress. It was a warm evening.

While they were driving, "How are mother and child?"

"Perfect in every way. Even though Lindsay's ready to leave the hospital, I think she's also scared about having to take care of the baby on her own."

"You'll be there."

"True. I think my daughter has discovered that her usual independent spirit may not be enough when it comes to being responsible for a tiny human. And to make things more complicated, my parents are arriving at dawn on Tuesday morning. Expecting to stay with me."

"But you don't have another bedroom."

"Which means I get the sectional." *A depressing prospect.* "Let's change the subject. Tell me about Sadie."

It seemed like forever since they'd shared a meal at the Brewery. Kara had a glass of white wine; Liam tried a new craft beer the waitress recommended. As usual, he had steak; Kara ordered shrimp. This felt like a date, certainly not a first date but not an after-work meal either. There was something different about Liam since he came back from North Carolina—lighter, more relaxed.

"Your sister sounded nice on the phone."

"She is nice—in an older sister, bossy way." He half smiled, "Her life's goal has always been to keep my head screwed on straight. She and Seth have two sons. Both of them are attending UNC in Charlotte, one's a senior, the other's a freshman. Once the boys were both in elementary school, Tracy started selling real estate. She mostly does it part-time. Her husband Seth teaches History at St. Augustine's University."

They skipped dessert, lingering over their drinks, neither ready for the evening to end, but Sadie had been confined to the cabin all evening. "She needs a walk or at least time outside. Do you have to get back right away?"

"No. I'll call Lindsay to make sure she's still coming home tomorrow."

Kara sat on the cabin steps while Liam took Sadie for a walk down the narrow driveway that ended on the main road into the ski area. She called Lindsay's cell. "Did I wake you?"

"No, I slept all afternoon. I just finished nursing Malia. It's lovely to do that, but no one mentioned that it also hurts."

"It'll get better. Did they give you a checkout time for tomorrow?"

"Eleven. I'm really glad you made me take your car to the fire station to have the child carrier put in. I can't take her home without it." *Points for Mom.*

Liam was walking back toward the cabin, "Okay then, I'll be there before eleven. Do you need me to bring anything?"

"I guess not."

"See you in the morning," she hit the red button. Sadie was nuzzling Kara's leg, wanting to be petted. "You're back to being pushy, I see." More nuzzling and more petting.

Sadie rode back to Kara's with them and, as soon as Kara got out of the car, Sadie jumped between the front seats and headed for the condo's front door. Liam reached for her leash. "Guess she's planning on going inside."

Once indoors, Sadie headed straight for the kitchen, disappointed there was no water bowl for her. Liam laughed. "She assumes your condo is her territory." Kara put water in a bowl for her and set it on the floor. "I'm so relieved she's healthy again that I've been spoiling her rather badly."

"We all spoil her, even Edgar, though he doesn't admit it."

They stood side-by-side watching Sadie splash water on the kitchen floor, Kara's arm so close to Liam's that her skin was tingling. She'd forgotten what wanting could do to her bones, turning them to liquid. Without a word, Liam put an arm around her, gently turning her so she was facing him and, with his hand on the back of her neck, began a long, searching kiss. Paused briefly, then more seriously pushed against her mouth, adding his tongue. Buried in her memory, Kara remembered serious kissing, letting herself match his urgency.

They were both short of breath when Liam smoothed her hair away from her face. "Are you—am I assuming too much?" His eyes hung onto hers, asking the question she hadn't imagined would ever be asked of her again. Mentally, she took herself off the shelf she'd been on.

"Keep assuming." She hadn't realized how much she had been wanting to feel his back beneath her hands, to feel his tongue in her mouth. Connecting to him in a way that had nothing to do with friendship or work or anything else except the two of them standing in the kitchen. Liam had seemed so closed off for all those months and now, with very little preamble, they were moving toward her bedroom.

She should have changed the sheets on her bed too. It hadn't occurred to her that they were ready for another kind of relationship. She'd been sleeping alone for nearly three years, been celibate, been okay with her own company. Did she want to fit him into her life? *Cut it out, Kara.* Clearly she was over-thinking what was happening. This was about enjoying the prospect of sex with a handsome, charming man. It wasn't like they were getting married.

Passion doesn't always involve frantically tearing off clothes. Slow can be exquisitely erotic. They slow-walked to the bedroom—hands and mouths exploring, anticipating. A gentle easing of Kara onto the bed. Liam joining her.

Outside the closed bedroom door, Sadie sighed and lay down. This was not a moment to complain about being excluded.

Chapter 18

Sadie barked them awake, sunlight already outlining the bedroom shutters. By the time Kara remembered why Sadie was in her condo, Liam was already pulling on his pants and leaving the bedroom. "Be right back."

Kara rolled onto her back, smiling at nothing in particular, savoring the lassitude that, for her, always followed sex—a silky well-being that made her middle-aged body feel like it was thirty. Last night had been—

She still hadn't finished the thought when Liam returned. "Sorry, but I didn't want to risk her having an accident inside. I left her in the patio." He sat on the edge of the bed and leaned over to kiss her. Softly, "Good morning."

"Good morning." *Good was definitely an understatement.*

"When do you have to leave for the hospital?"

"Ummm, maybe ten-thirty." The clock on the nightstand showed almost nine-thirty. "Guess I need to get my act together." *Good luck with that.* She would need more than an hour to find the pieces of herself that had been so expertly rearranged last night.

"I'll use the guest bathroom. Do you have a toothbrush I can appropriate? I seem to have come unprepared." His grin suggested so many things.

"Check the cabinet under the sink."

As soon as he left the room, Kara hurried into her bathroom. Being naked in the dark and beneath covers was one thing, daylight nakedness, at her age, quite another. The younger generation would laugh at her discomfort.

She was adding fresh raspberries to her cold cereal when Liam came into the kitchen, unshaven, his hair still damp. "I've never tried the scruffy look before." He was rubbing his hand over the stubble along his jaw.

It made him even better looking. "Not bad, but won't it itch?"

"No doubt. I should carry toiletries in my car."

So he was planning on other nights?

Just where did she want this new dimension in their relationship to go? For that matter where did he want it to go? She already felt—different. With him. Good different. The easy rapport they'd established working together had morphed into a charged awareness. She was foolishly attempting to be rational about long-forgotten emotions that had invaded her head.

But the real world called.

"I need to run. Lindsay is already nervous about today. My being late will not help. What are you and Sadie doing?"

"I hadn't anticipated this, us—and well, I have an appointment tomorrow in Santa Fe with my lawyer. I set it up before I came for the reception. The rights to some of the photos I took a decade ago are reverting to me. I want my lawyer to review the details before I sign the documents. So we're going to Pecos."

Disappointment swept over her.

On the other hand, she couldn't or shouldn't repeat last night while her daughter was staying with her. And in two days, her parents would arrive. That event she could certainly do without.

"So I won't see you for a while."

"A few days." He put his arms around her, kissed her, then took her right hand and placed a key in it. "In case you want some peace and quiet, this is the key to the cabin. You might want to hide out. The Museum won't care." He smiled. "Don't worry. I'm not going to France."

Kara arrived at the hospital on time but, because she stopped to sign the paperwork at the front desk, she was fifteen minutes late getting to Lindsay's room. Her daughter was sitting in a wheelchair—required for exiting the building—holding the baby. "You're late."

Not a good opening. Any other day, Kara might have been defensive, but nothing—not even her daughter—was going to ruin the way she felt this morning. "I had to sign you out."

A nurse hurried in, "All ready?" She took the handles of the wheelchair. To Kara, "Can you manage her bag?"

Kara followed them and, once outside, led the way to her car. It took another fifteen minutes for Kara and Lindsay to make sure Malia was properly settled in the car seat. Lindsay rode in back to keep an eye on her daughter.

Overseeing Lindsay's first day of mothering prevented any ruminating about Liam and last night and, well, everything. Hard to imagine that a three-day old baby could fill up the condo, but she did. Though they'd only purchased a bassinet and a changing table, there were disposable diapers and wipes, the container for the diapers, receiving blankets, baby powder, onesies, etc. etc. The guest room and second bathroom were running over with baby paraphernalia.

Everything was centered on feeding Malia, changing Malia, bathing her in the kitchen sink, feeding her—repeat and repeat. At least, when Kara had been helping out with Camden, Jeff was there as back-up. He and Ellen had, after all, dealt with newborns before. Lindsay however was new at this, nervous about everything, vacillating between whiny and joyous.

Late that afternoon, Lindsay took a shower, asking pointedly why there was a damp towel on the back of the bathroom door. Kara ignored the question, taking the trash outside, then staying to water the plants in the patio. Fortunately, the subject didn't recur.

She was too tired to fix dinner for herself and Lindsay, so she ordered lasagna and salad from Olive Garden and went to bed early, letting herself remember the previous night in sweet detail.

Malia woke them at midnight.

In Pecos, Liam and Sadie were sitting in the living room, staring at the empty wall where the French photographs had hung. Reminders of his past—admittedly a good one—but he couldn't keep living in both then and now. Dr. Elaine had used a rather weird analogy. *Eating three meals yesterday doesn't remove the necessity of eating today. If you never ate again, because of those three meals, you would starve. That's what you're doing, Liam, starving your emotional self. There's nothing noble about depriving yourself.*

He asked Sadie if she missed the photos but only heard a mild snuffle. He asked himself the same question. The answer was pending.

Over all these months, Kara had been moving into the edges of his life, and the night before, she had moved closer to the center. In his post-married existence, this was the first time sex hadn't been just a one or two-night stand. This time, with Kara, was more than physical desire; there was a sense of belonging. Deliberate and deep. Asking him to be more than he'd been in a long time.

As a result, he was terrified. Maybe he should stay in Pecos longer than he'd planned.

Because Malia's night involved spells of crying, Kara and Lindsay were both short on sleep and, perversely, the baby was now sleeping soundly. Kara was tempted to keep her awake so she'd sleep during the night. Probably not good grandparenting. After breakfast, Lindsay fell asleep in the living room while Kara began a grocery list, a long one since there would soon be two more mouths to feed. She couldn't put clean sheets on her bed until tomorrow, probably after her parents' 6 a.m. arrival. Welcome to Hotel Kara.

The doorbell interrupted her.

On the doorstep was a tall, muscular young man, maybe thirty, warm dark skin and curly black hair, wearing a multi-colored Hawaiian shirt. "Hi. I'm Max. I'm assuming Lindsay and my brand new daughter are here." *Still no last name.*

Hotel Kara was completely booked.

"I'm Lindsay's mother, Kara. She didn't tell me you were coming."

"She doesn't know." He picked up his bright blue duffle bag and followed her into the hallway. "As soon as she texted about the baby, I got a flight from Perth, to Hawaii and then to Phoenix. I've lost all sense of time."

In a stage whisper so as not to wake the baby, "Max! You're here!" A half-awake Lindsay, tousled hair and no make up, threw her arms around him.

Kara discreetly escaped to the kitchen.

Depending on the outcome of his unannounced appearance, Kara just might need to use the cabin key Liam had given her. And even if Max weren't relegated to the sectional, by tomorrow there would be too many people using two bathrooms, and Kara would undoubtedly be the last in line.

In the kitchen, she leaned on the counter and studied the half-finished grocery list. Feeding five adults would require more food than she had on hand. And additional cash. She usually didn't charge groceries, but this might be the day. She hadn't earned anything for the last five months, getting by on the small payouts from her Merrill Lynch account. Fortunately, Lindsay was being paid during her maternity leave, so she bought all the baby supplies. Kara might soon need help with the household expenses. She didn't want to go into her capital if she could help it.

Half an hour later, Malia's parents were sitting on the sectional, staring at their sleeping daughter. Kara grabbed her purse and paused in the doorway, "I'm going to the store," and didn't wait for a response.

Off duty.

And outside. She didn't even mind that it was still summer-hot. Before going to the store, she stopped at the gas station and filled the tank, then drove to the cabin to see if there were clean sheets. She certainly seemed to be dealing with sheets a lot lately. Quite possibly she would be sleeping there tomorrow night.

Lindsay thought she was dreaming when she heard Max's voice. But he was real, standing in her mother's front hall. She threw herself into his arms like a lovesick idiot. She didn't mind that her mother was watching. "Come see our daughter." She pulled him into the living room and stopped beside the bassinet on the coffee table.

"Malia, this is your daddy."

His eyes suddenly tearing, Max reached into the bassinet to touch her miniature fingers; "She's beautiful."

"Wait until she cries all night."

"Was labor hard?"

"Yeah. Thank heavens, she was in a hurry so it didn't last too long."

"I love her name."

"Since she looks Hawaiian, I thought it fit."

"What's her middle name?"

"I couldn't come up with one."

"So what's on her birth certificate?"

"Malia NMI Talmadge."

"Not Akanu?"

Lindsay switched to defensive mode. "You weren't here so we could talk about it. And we're not married. Besides, I hate hyphenated names."

Perhaps sensing trouble in the air, Malia woke up and let out a wail. Max gave a short laugh, "Wow. Strong lungs. She'll be a good swimmer."

Lindsay picked her up, rocking her gently, but Malia did not stop crying.

"Can I hold her?"

"Good luck. She's probably hungry."

He took her from Lindsay. In their first father/daughter moment, Malia got quiet. He walked her around the living room, "Hello baby girl. Would you like to surf? I can teach you."

Lindsay watched, quietly amazed at what was happening. She hadn't been able to stop Malia's wailing in any way other than feeding her. Max however was working magic. She shouldn't be surprised. He was capable of working magic on her too. Bringing out her better self.

When Kara returned, Lindsay was sitting on the sectional, Malia at her breast and Max alongside, watching intently. An iPhone moment, but her iPhone was in the car with her purse and the rest of the groceries.

Max stood up. "Do you have more in the car?"

Kara nodded. "And a basket of laundry." Might as well put him to good use.

By the time the Amtrak from Los Angeles pulled into Flagstaff's train station Tuesday morning, Kara had pretty much decided Max was good for her daughter. Lindsay was a different person with him-—gracious, gentle, no edge—and he was definitely smitten by his baby daughter. It was fun to watch them being new parents. But now the great-grandparents were entering the picture. They hadn't seen Lindsay since Michael's memorial service and hadn't known about Lindsay's pregnancy until she was four or five months along. Her mother would now be the one to ask the questions Kara hadn't asked. A rather satisfactory arrangement.

There were more people on the station platform than Kara expected. It took her a few minutes to locate her parents. Her father, no longer six feet tall, his hair thin and gray, was harder to find in the crowd. Each parent pulled a roll-on suitcase and both looked as though they hadn't slept much since leaving San Jose.

She reached her mother first, dropping a quick kiss on her cheek, more wrinkled than the last time she'd seen her, and taking the suitcase handle. "How was your trip?"

Before her mother answered, her father reached them, "Making the connection in LA was so confusing. I thought we might miss our train. They need more signs."

Kara kissed him. "But here you are, safe and sound."

"Are you parked close by?"

"Right out front. Follow me." Kara automatically slowed her usual pace. Neither of her parents had ever walked fast. Not a good idea to out-walk them when they were already tired. She felt herself tense up. It was going to be hard having four generations in the same house, and she was the one responsible for managing all their personalities.

Before they reached her car, she was already looking forward to sleeping at the cabin.

Chapter 19

That afternoon, Liam called Kara but ended up in her voicemail.

I know you're busy with family. I'm about to have Tracy on my doorstep. She suddenly decided to visit and is flying into Albuquerque tomorrow, then coming to Flag with me on Friday to see the show. So I'll be here longer. How are you?

Seriously overwhelmed!

Not a word she liked to use since the younger generation had made it their go-to explanation for everything. Given her current circumstances however, no other word fit. Thank God for Max. When she and her parents arrived at the condo, Lindsay was sleeping in the guest room. Max had the bassinet in the kitchen where he was making coffee and frying bacon. "We're letting Mommy sleep in." He looked right at home.

"Max, these are my parents. Simon and Valerie. This is Max and your great- granddaughter, Malia."

Her mother eagerly bent over the bassinet, then, with a hint of surprise, "She has dark skin."

An embarrassing moment. It had never occurred to Kara to tell her parents that Malia's father was mostly Hawaiian. Their generation would assume their fair-skinned granddaughter would have a fair-skinned baby. To his credit, Max simply grinned. "Just like me."

Kara liked him even more.

To change the conversation, "Let me show you your room." Kara took her mother's suitcase and exited the kitchen. Before she left for the train station, she'd changed the sheets on her bed, dusted, and wiped down the bathroom. It might be a cliché, but women always wanted their houses in good order when their mothers visited. That paranoia never disappeared.

It was late afternoon before Kara had time to call Liam. She took her cell to her car so no one could overhear. She was looking forward to talking to him.

He answered on the second ring. "Hi."

"Hi." Not brilliant conversation.

"Everything okay?"

"What do you want to hear first, the good or the awkward?"

"I'll take the good to help me face the awkward." He seemed to be teasing her. She relaxed.

"Max arrived yesterday and is truly a wonder. He cooked breakfast for my parents, will hardly let Malia out of his sight, changes diapers like a pro, and my daughter is a totally different person with him."

"Diapers, eh? How'd that happen?"

"According to Max, younger brothers and sisters."

"Okay, let's have the awkward."

"The first words out of my mother's mouth when she saw Malia were *She has dark skin.* Max didn't turn a hair but I was embarrassed. My father has taken to worrying about every little thing, and I can see my mother watching him out of the corner of her eye all the time. As though he needs her supervision. Max slept on the sectional and kept the bassinet with him so Lindsay only had to wake up to feed the baby. Anyway, I'm sleeping at the cabin tonight. I made up the bed in the back bedroom." She paused, "What made Tracy decide to visit?"

"She always gives me trouble for not visiting her, so I gave her the same kind of trouble. Since my younger nephew is away at college this year, she and Seth have an empty nest. Bottom line, she ran out of excuses."

"Should I clear out of the cabin on Friday?" Her parents weren't going home until Sunday. If Max was still on the sectional, things were going to get complicated. Sleeping on the floor in her own house or making Max sleep there were not good options.

"The cabin has three bedrooms. Enough to go around."

No sharing this time.

"Okay." Safe subject: "How's Sadie?"

"Happy to be home."

Perhaps Liam was happy to be there too.

After they said goodbye, she stayed in the car for a while, realizing that they had reverted to their comfortably platonic *friendship*. No hint they'd slept together. She'd hoped for—more. He didn't say he missed her. She'd obviously given that night more importance than she should have. It felt as though he'd pulled away. So quickly.

Her parents managed to stay awake until they'd had lunch and then used the afternoon to catch up on their sleep. Max engineered dinner. Nothing fancy, hamburgers and frozen French fries, but at least Kara didn't have to cook. He was accumulating more brownie points.

Because Max was helping out with Malia, Lindsay was forced to spend time talking to her grandparents, fending off questions like: *when are you getting married, are you going to stay in Hawaii?* Max jumped in to explain the surfing enterprise in Australia, temporarily keeping Valerie's tough questions at bay.

Everyone except Kara and Max were in bed by nine o'clock. Malia was fussing and Kara was walking her back and forth in the kitchen while Max took a shower in Kara's bathroom so he wouldn't disturb Lindsay. Her parents slept through his shower.

He reappeared barefooted, wearing what were probably surfing shorts and a bright green *Hilo Howls* t-shirt. "Want me to take her?"

"Please. I need to put together a few things for overnight. I'm going out to the cabin that the Museum owns. I'll be back in the morning. Can you manage everyone? It's kind of an instant immersion into the family."

"No problem. I come from a big, rather unruly family."

"Are your parents in Hawaii?"

"My mom passed when I was in high school. My dad three years ago. Brothers, sisters, aunts and uncles scattered throughout the islands." He took Malia from her. "My phone is on the counter in the kitchen. Would you mind entering your cell number in case I do need help?"

"Of course."

When she was ready to leave, she stopped in the living room where Max and Malia were cuddling. The baby was silently awake. A first.

"She is so calm with you."

"I know. I'm already her slave."

"Do you mind my asking how long you'll be here? Lindsay would kill me if she knew I asked."

He smiled, "She is touchy about some things. I'm flying back to Australia on Monday, and I'm not looking forward to that flight. Crossing the dateline does strange things to my body."

He hadn't mentioned whether Lindsay was staying or going with him— but at least Kara had part of her answer. "See you tomorrow."

She slept a full seven hours. The cabin was so blessedly quiet Kara was tempted to stay the whole day, but the potential fallout from her playing hooky wasn't worth it. She showered and washed her hair, stopped to pick up coffee before returning to the mini chaos that had invaded her living space. Surprisingly, the house was quiet. The new parents were taking Malia to her check up appointment with Dr. Angelo. Val was in the kitchen, watching the *Today* program on the small TV Kara kept on the kitchen counter; and her father was sitting on the patio, reading a book—a very thick book.

"What's Dad reading?"

"Something about President Grant. The book weighs a ton, but he's obsessed with it. He went outside, claiming the TV was too distracting."

"Have you guys had breakfast?"

"Long ago. The baby was up at five and so were the rest of us. She's adorable but I forget that a baby controls everything in a household."

And this was only the first week.

Instead of sitting around the house with her parents, Kara decided to play tour guide. After all, they had never been to Flagstaff. "Would you and Dad like to see the Museum show that I was helping out with? Maybe have lunch in town."

"Doesn't someone need to be here for the baby?"

"She has her parents. Lindsay's a little iffy about the whole bath and diaper routine, but I think Max can handle it." It shouldn't take five people to watch over a six day old baby who only ate and slept.

Valerie switched off the TV. "I'd like to go. I don't know whether we can separate your father from his book."

In the two plus years since Kara had seen her parents, they seemed to have become elderly. Small differences. Both needed more time to get into and out of the car, and she found herself having to repeat things for her mother.

Maddy was on duty at the Museum and smiled as soon as Kara and her parents entered the lobby. "I've been meaning to call. How's the baby?" She noticed Simon and Valerie behind Kara. "Oh, you've brought guests. Hi, welcome to the Museum."

Kara made the introductions and reached for her wallet to pay the entrance fees.

"Oh don't. You work here, or will be working next month." They're your guests. She handed each a brochure. "You'll love the portraits."

As they entered the gallery, the motion-activated lights went on, instantly bringing the artists to life. Though Kara had been involved in creating the show, the impact of the photos that encircled the hall made her catch her breath. "Take your time; I'll be back in a few minutes."

Kara returned to the lobby to talk to Maddy. "They'll be fine for a bit. So nice to see you."

"How are mother and child, Malia is it?"

"Yes. They're surprisingly good if you ignore Lindsay's sleep deprivation. Has the rumor mill mentioned that Malia's daddy showed up? Max."

"No. Is this the first time you've met him? What does he look like?"

Kara pulled her phone out and located the photos she'd taken of the young family.

"Wow, he's a hunk."

Kara laughed, "Yeah," then retold the story about her mother being shocked that the baby had darkish skin. "My folks seem to like Max, but then what's not to like? And he's great at taking care of the baby. He had younger siblings."

"Is Lindsay staying here or going back with him?"

"I doubt she's ready to fly that far. It's a really long trip for a newborn, and I understand some airlines want babies to be at least two months old before they can fly. Currently, Max is sleeping on the sectional and keeping the baby with him in case she wakes. If she wants food, he wakes Lindsay. They seem to be managing without my oversight."

"So where are you sleeping?"

"The cabin. Liam is in Pecos."

"Is he now," Maddy grinned. "The rumor mill missed the Max story, but it has reported that Liam went to the hospital the night the baby was born and was seen taking you home."

Though she knew Maddy was teasing, Kara hoped she wasn't blushing.

"His sister is meeting him in Pecos and then the two of them are driving here."

"Have you met her?"

"No, I talked to her on the phone a couple of times." She glanced at the clock on the wall, "I need to get back to my folks." Talking about Liam was not comfortable.

There were now several other people in the gallery and Val, true to form, was busy telling them that her daughter had been part of this project and had met every one of the people in the photos. Michael always said that, if you put Val into a room with people she'd just encountered, she would have talked to all of them within the hour and know all about them even though she had no idea what their names were.

And it was, once again, true. Her father was off to one side quietly studying the photos. He wasn't much on outreach.

Kara came up behind him. "Do you like them?"

"They're quite powerful. Whoever this Liam Kincaid is, he knows how to capture their souls."

"He does. It was amazing to watch him work. And each of the subjects was so interesting to talk to. I loved being part of this." It was the first time, other than the day the pictures were hung, that she'd felt the full effect of the show. "I was sorry to miss the reception. Some of the artists came in their native dress. I was looking forward to seeing them again, but Lindsay was busy becoming a mother. We start on a new, but smaller group of artists the first week in October."

"Do I have time to look at the Museum Shop?"

"Plenty of time. We can do whatever you want. Later, I'll drive you around town."

"Are you happy here?"

"Yes." Mostly.

They told Val where they were going and left her to her new friends.

After lunch, Kara drove them by the cabin, "My temporary camping spot," then drove by the art store while she explained about the art class that would begin after New Year's. She showed them where Jeff's family had lived, the building he worked in.

"So Jeff just up and moved."

"Yes."

"And then wanted you to go there to help out with the new baby?"

"Yes." Defending the situation or attacking it would accomplish nothing.

Taking a detour, Val asked, "How are you doing financially?"

Safer territory. "Hanging on. Many things are cheaper here than in LA. Michael's law office will be paying off the full amount of the note, so I'll be getting a monthly check from the brokerage account, and I'll be back working at the Museum for about six weeks.

"Eventually I need to have something steady. I might even see if I can finish my degree. The units from UCLA are thirty years old so they might not be usable. If I finish, I could maybe teach art part time in elementary schools, but that's a long shot. I might be able to get back on at the Museum—sometime."

"I don't suppose Jeff can help out. I mean, he must be making good money."

"And has three children. Ellen isn't working now."

Moving on to Lindsay, her mother wanted to know whether Lindsay and Max were going to get married. Kara didn't know. Whether Lindsay was going back to Hawaii or going to Australia. Or staying in Flagstaff. Kara didn't know.

"Don't the two of you ever talk?"

"You're welcome to ask her all those questions. She's not always forthcoming with me."

"Ah well, neither were you at that age."

The joy of family baggage.

On Thursday, everyone, even the baby, went to Sedona for an early dinner. Since the baby seat was in Kara's car, Malia went with Kara and Val, while Max, Lindsay and Simon rode in Max's rental. The baby's first day out in the wider world and she slept through most of her adventure. Thankfully, she didn't disrupt the people in the restaurant.

Tomorrow, Liam and his sister would arrive. Kara was uneasy about Liam. Having sex had not brought them closer—it was as if that kind of intimacy had scared him away.

Chapter 20

Tracy hadn't been in the Southwest since her father's death nearly thirteen years ago. She'd forgotten how dry the vegetation was, especially in early fall before the winter rains arrived. Muted gray-greens instead of the vivid East Coast green, but she still loved the rough sage and pungent dryness. Sky everywhere. The day after she arrived, she and Liam drove to Colorado to visit Allison, where they grew up. Having lost its post office decades ago, now it was little more than a wide spot in the road. Only a small Presbyterian church beside the highway. Gradually, the small ranches in the area had been absorbed by commercial operations. After Rob Kincaid died, the adjacent, corporation-owned ranch had bought his property. Their one-story frame bungalow was still at the end of the gravel driveway, probably housing someone who worked on the ranch.

Tracy was leaning against the back of Liam's SUV, her digital camera pointed at the house and the San Juan Mountains in the distance. "I'm sure the boys don't remember anything about this place. Nick was in elementary school the last time we were here. The house could use a coat of paint." She slid the camera into its case. "I always forget that the wind never stops blowing. I guess we didn't pay attention to uncomfortable weather when we were young."

They drove west to Ignacio for lunch. It was the first time Tracy had seen the town where they'd gone to school since the casino and several multi-story hotels had been built. "It looks like a Las Vegas wanna-be," she complained.

Liam agreed. The whole *you shouldn't go home again* issue.

After dinner at Liam's cabin, Tracy took Sadie on a walk, though what she really wanted to do was sit Liam down and poke around in his psyche, find out what he was really thinking, if the therapy had changed anything. But she knew full well he wasn't going to share his feelings with her. She often wondered whether he'd ever completely shared himself with Ariane or if it was her death that locked him up.

Tracy had liked her sister-in-law though they'd seldom spent much time together. Ariane had only been to Raleigh two or three times in the eleven years she and Liam were married. Two very different women who loved the same man. Liam and Ariane were amazing together. Strong and successful, enjoying their glamorous lifestyle.

Until the crash.

Tracy could still hear her brother's shattered voice, his despair, the afternoon he called for her help. A man drowning. She could only sort out the practical matters for him. There was no way to console him. In the years since, they had never talked about those days or about her and Seth accompanying Liam and the caskets to France for the Mass in Roussillon. An entire village grieving. Ariane's family and friends hugging Liam, who stood stiffly in their warm embraces. Unable or unwilling to accept their condolences or recognize that they were grieving too.

That coolness—maybe coldness—had stayed during his months in Europe. He was drinking too much, letting Tracy dispose of the apartment and everything in it. Shutting down his photographic career. Eventually, checking himself into a rehab facility. Not until he moved to New Mexico did he begin to climb out of the abyss. He had a new house, Sadie, and now the job with the Museum. He was closer to being the brother she'd once known. Where Kara figured into this resurrection Tracy had no idea. Liam hadn't mentioned her. Not easy to ask him what was going on or, more realistically, what wasn't going on.

She did venture what she thought was a safe question. "How come you don't have anything hanging on that wall?" She pointed. "It needs something, considering the ceiling is vaulted."

"I recently took down what was there."

"What did you have there? Some of your work?"

"Four large black and white photos."

"And?"

"And I'm trying not to need them anymore. I put them in the shed."

Before she could probe further, he'd escaped to the front porch with Sadie.

The subject didn't resurface on their drive to Flagstaff the next afternoon.

It was nearly eleven o'clock Friday night when Kara let herself into the Museum's cabin; the living room was lit by one small lamp. Her bedroom door was open but the other two were closed. Obviously Liam had given up on her. She checked her texts and found a brief message: **We're turning in. See you tomorrow.** She was late because her parents wanted the family to play Canasta. They loved games, and Kara didn't have the heart to leave even though she wanted to see Liam and meet Tracy.

When Kara walked into the kitchen the next morning, Tracy was wiping down the kitchen counter. "Good morning. I'm Kara. I didn't intend to get in so late last night. Where are Liam and Sadie?"

Tracy crossed the room to give Kara a hug and kiss her cheek. "I'm so glad to finally meet you. There's coffee and one croissant left. Liam and Sadie are at the Museum. He wanted to set up something for the next project."

What could be so important at this hour of the morning?

It felt like he was intentionally avoiding her.

"Just coffee, thanks. I need to get back to my place."

"Liam's going to pick me up later so I can see the show in the gallery. He's very proud of it."

"It really is wonderful. He did terrific work."

"Can you join us? I'd love to have both of you with me when I see it for the first time."

"Sorry. This is the last day my parents are here, and my mother wants to do some shopping. They have to catch the train at 8:10 tomorrow morning. How long will you be here?"

"Until Tuesday. Since I'm this close to LA, I'm taking the train to visit a college friend I haven't seen in years."

Tracy was easy to talk to. One cup of coffee became two, and finally Kara ate the croissant because she was starving. They shared cell phone pictures of their children. Tracy recounted the trip to their childhood home, simultaneously wondering whether she could ask, carefully, if Kara and Liam were a couple, Kara wondering whether she could ask if Liam had talked about her.

Tracy took a circuitous route. "Do you think Liam has changed since he came back from North Carolina? I mean you two worked pretty closely before he went to New York."

Kara was equally cautious. "At first, yes. I thought he was more relaxed, more accessible."

"But?"

"Since he returned to Pecos, he hasn't been communicating." Never a good sign with him.

"When he left Raleigh last month, I thought he'd really begun to move on. But I sense something has changed again."

Kara wanted to say *Changed, as in slept with me. And it sent him running.*

Instead of telling Tracy what the cause probably was, she excused herself to take her mother shopping. At least, Liam's retreat wasn't just her imagination.

Not until late that night, did Liam and Kara cross paths. He apologized for not having the time to meet her parents, asked about the baby. All very correct. The three of them finished off the Ben and Jerry's ice cream that Tracy had bought, talked about the new photo project, and went to bed. In very separate rooms. The next morning, Kara left at 4 a.m. to wake her parents and get them to the train station. Neither Tracy nor Liam made an appearance.

No one needed to tell Liam he was, once again, emotionally on the run and, this time, was hurting Kara by shutting down what had begun between them. He'd briefly removed the wall he'd built around himself. But without the wall, he was again vulnerable to the kind of pain that had kept him paralyzed since Ariane's death.

Kara was the first woman since Ariane that he wanted to spend time with, to make love to. He might even be on the cusp of loving her. That realization let the panic in. The possibility of another loss would not go away.

Dr. Elaine had thrown the word *fear* at him. She was right.

Avoidance was his preferred protection but Tracy caught him out when they were waiting for her train on Tuesday afternoon.

"I like Kara. Why are you avoiding her?"

"I'm not."

"Liar. Other than sharing ice cream the other night, you've hardly seen her. You were in bed before she came to the cabin, up and gone before she got up. You haven't gone to her place and didn't meet her parents."

"I'm glad you like her. I thought you would."

"That's not my point and you know it. What happened?"

Liam considered his options and then reverted to being twelve. "None of your business."

The train's warning horn sounded in the distance. For Tracy, it was now or never. "You slept with her. Am I right? And then you ran back to Pecos. I bet you didn't have an appointment with a lawyer."

Sisters never stopped being a pain. "Did too."

"Liam Kincaid, you're a scairdy cat."

"Am not."

"Are too." And now she was twelve.

The train glided silently into the station, silver and sleek. Doors opened, passengers exited.

She put her arms around Liam and held him tightly against her. "I love you little brother. I love your photographs and I think you should let yourself love Kara. But if not her, please find someone who will make you happy."

Before he could say anything, she handed her ticket to the conductor and disappeared into the car.

Five minutes later, the train slid silently away from the station, leaving Liam wishing she wasn't right.

For Kara there was too little to do and too much empty space.
Her parents were back in San Jose.

Max was enroute to Western Australia.

Tracy was in LA.

Only Lindsay and Malia remained.

A week later, the new photo project got underway. The scheduling was tighter than the first time around as Edgar planned to finish by Thanksgiving. Liam and Kara slipped back into their roles: photographer and assistant. It was as though they had never had sex, had never shared the night that she kept remembering. He was last year's Liam: casual, friendly, appreciative of her help during the photo sessions. Gracious with the artists. But there were no lunches or dinners and certainly no touching. No enticing undercurrents.

She was hurt. More than hurt. *Pissed.* She'd always heard the term, one-night stand but never imagined she would be one. Another woman might confront him and demand to know why he'd changed his mind about her—but she was afraid of knowing why. As Lindsay had observed all too accurately, *You just go along with what someone else wants you to do.*

Or in this case not do again.

So when Lindsay asked Kara if she would accompany her and Malia to Hilo, to help on the plane trip, Kara said yes. The baby was almost two months old; the noise and strangeness of an airplane could be a perfect catalyst for mega-crying. Malia didn't need much to set her off anyway. A grandmother would be useful. Lindsay would be paying Kara's fare, conveniently allowing her to put geographical distance between herself and the distance Liam had brought to their relationship.

Kara assumed Lindsay wanted to get herself established in Hilo before she had to return to work the first of the year, but she was wrong. Lindsay and Max had decided what Lindsay and Malia would do before he returned to Australia. As usual, Lindsay hadn't shared.

"I'm going to apply for leave from the school district. I don't think there will be a problem since I have tenure. Max and I agreed that Malia and I should go to Perth, stay there until the training program is up and running in the spring. Then Max is going to set up a smaller version of the program in Hilo. Maybe next year."

"When do we leave?" Kara did have to make a few arrangements, stop the mail, and assure the art store she would only be gone for a week or so.

"If I can get tickets, next Sunday. I need to find Malia's birth certificate. Once we're in Hawaii, I'll get both of us passports and Australian visas."

Lindsay was excited. She missed Max and Hawaii. She hurried around for the next few days, figuring out what she could and couldn't take on the plane for Malia and texting Max several times a day. Kara told Edgar that she would be gone for the last two artists' sittings. "My daughter needs another pair of hands for the trip to Hilo. Should I also alert Chet?" Once again, she was walking away from her job at the Museum. They might never rehire her—for anything. Hopefully, the art classes would fill up in January, and her cash flow should improve. Edith planned to begin advertising the classes after Thanksgiving.

Liam took the news that she wouldn't be finishing the project almost too well. Most of the developing and printing was completed and only two more artists were on the schedule.

He was politely interested in what Lindsay and Max were going to do. Pleased that Kara could help during the flight and then have a mini vacation. He asked all the right questions, assured her he could manage.

But she did not want him to manage!

She wanted him to say he was sorry to see her go, to kiss her tenderly and tell her she mattered to him. Her throat was so tight she couldn't risk asking what he would do next.

Settling for, "Give Sadie my love."

On her way home from the Museum, tears coursed down her cheeks, making for hazardous driving. Until she could see the road clearly, she pulled into a shopping mall parking lot.

Crying for a man who would never be able to let another woman into his life.

Chapter 21

The last time Kara was in Hawaii, she and Michael were attending Lindsay's graduation from the university in Honolulu. They spent most of their time in the city, not seeing the Oahu backcountry or the waves on the North Shore. One morning they had, however, gone out to visit the *Arizona* Memorial.

She'd never been to Hilo. From the air, Hawaii's Big Island was a canvas of green and black, lava and vegetation competing for control. Hilo didn't have many high rises, just looming volcanoes in its backyard. During Kilauea's eruption last year, Kara had worried about Lindsay, but her daughter had downplayed any danger. "I'm on the other side of the city."

As the plane made its approach into Hilo International, Kara wasn't so sure just how safe Lindsay had been. Kilauea, now quiet, seemed alarmingly close to the city. Kara could see the wide scars where the lava had buried whole neighborhoods. Today, however, the sky was clear, no steam rising, the lush tropical vegetation pushing against the freshly cooled lava, creating an abstract design along the ocean. Lindsay had assured her the water temperature would be in the high seventies. Warmer than Southern California's water.

Ironically, Nana's services hadn't been needed on the plane trip. After take off, which is notoriously hard on a baby's ears, Malia quickly calmed down and slept for the next three hours. After Lindsay fed her, Malia went back to sleep. It did, however, take both of them to manage the baby, the car seat, the diaper bag, and suitcases. Taking a baby anywhere was a major logistical operation. The taxi that delivered them to Max's small house was filled to the brim. The bungalow, with gray siding, blue trimmed windows, and a metal roof, was on the north side of Hilo, its front yard currently a mini-jungle. Neglected and forlorn.

"It looks better when the grass is cut. I didn't think to pay the gardener ahead. He's a friend of Max's so he'll probably come sort out the yard as soon as I call."

The taxi driver carried their bags to the front porch. Lindsay settled the bill and tipped him while Kara held the car seat with Malia, who was beginning to wake up. Fussing herself toward crying. They wrestled everything into the living room, which was crowded with wicker furniture upholstered in colorful, mismatched fabrics. The walls were covered with surfing posters from around the world. Max's decorating style was bachelor-minimalist.

"How old is the house?"

"No idea, but it belonged to his parents. Imagine a big family living here. Three bedrooms, very small bedrooms, this living room, and a kitchen that borders on primitive. But there's also a covered lanai out back. People in Hawaii live outdoors as much as they can, so it's kind of a family room. The best part of this place is it's free and clear. Max gradually paid off his brothers and sisters' shares since none of them wanted it. He's the oldest but he's the only one still single." She looked at the baby, "Oops, she's awake."

Malia sharply reminded them she was in need of a clean diaper and milk. Kara left Lindsay to it and chose one of the small bedrooms to unpack her suitcase.

Over the Thanksgiving weekend, the weather was wet and warm, the temperatures in the eighties; rain every day—but not all day. Kara didn't get in as much swimming as she'd imagined. November, it turns out, is one of Hawaii's wettest months. Since Max's house was close to the main part of town, Kara could walk to the shops and stop for coffee. Playing tourist.

Lindsay surfed the morning after they arrived, like an addict who had been deprived of a fix and, depending on the surf, was in the water at least twice a day. The rest of the time was spent skyping with Max, running errands, and obtaining passports and Australian visas.

"Max is coming at Christmas, and we'll go back to Perth with him. I need to figure out what Malia and I will need. I'm sure I can buy baby stuff in Perth, but I'm still going to take as much as I can." Kara was amazed at how fast Lindsay had gone from a fearful new mother to one who was careful about what she bought for Malia's care.

"Where does he live?"

"Right now, in a dorm with the staff, but he's got a lead on an apartment for us."

End of shared information. Kara did get to meet the young women Lindsay had lived with and see the school where she taught. "The school board granted me leave through June. I have to pay out-of-pocket to keep my health care since Max doesn't have benefits. We need to figure out how that will work in Australia." And again, there was the adult Lindsay. Kara needed to stop being surprised. Seeing her daughter in her own setting was encouraging. Lindsay really was surprisingly capable of taking care of Malia and sorting out their move to Australia.

Other than minding Malia when Lindsay was surfing or shopping, Kara didn't have anything to do. On the outside of Lindsay's life, looking in. Just like Cincinnati with Jeff's family. And since Max would soon be back, it was time to go home. Kara checked on flights to Phoenix and made a reservation. Lindsay, again, supplied her credit card.

When Kara got home, Liam would undoubtedly be back in Pecos, leaving an empty space in her life. She reminded herself that she shouldn't spend any more time wondering whether he would ever move past his feelings for Ariane. Talk about chasing the wrong rainbow.

"Is Liam still in Flagstaff?"

"No idea. But the photo sittings were finished two days ago, so I suppose he's retreated to Pecos."

"He seems like a nice guy."

High praise after Lindsay's initial attitude in April.

"Yes he is."

"Is anything going to come of it?" *It* covered a multitude of meanings.

Kara did not want to have this conversation. "I doubt it." She headed for her bedroom. "Since I'm leaving tomorrow, I'm going for one last swim."

Lindsay's voice followed her. "Dad's been gone a while. I don't think you should pass on Liam."

And so now she was matchmaking?

"I'm not the one doing the passing. He's passing on anyone who isn't his dead wife." A harsh exit line, but way too true.

Accept it.

153

Kara ordered a taxi to take her to the Hilo airport. No sense transporting Malia, just to say goodbye. It would be months until she saw her daughter and granddaughter again. While the taxi was waiting at the curb, she and Lindsay teared up. "Thanks for helping, Mom. I know I dumped myself on you."

"You're welcome. Thanks for paying my way." About as close to warm and fuzzy as they were likely to get. Being with Lindsay in Hilo had taken some of the kinks out of Kara's brain, helping her get ready to start the art classes in January. They would keep her mind off Liam's absence. Give her some direction. Maybe it was time to finish her degree.

While Liam was cleaning up the studio after the final sitting, Maddy knocked on the doorframe. "Can I ask you something or would later be better?"

"Now is fine."

"Would you mind showing my son JT a few basics about your 4" x 5" camera? He's really interested in photography, not the digital kind, using an iPhone like most of his friends, but the old-fashioned kind like you do. He's been to see the Plateau show three times. Just tell me if it's too much trouble."

"No trouble at all. When does he get out of school?"

"Three o'clock."

"Can he get himself here when he's finished?"

"Yes. He has a truck and a two-month old driver's license." Maddy's usually placid expression vanished for a moment. "I worry. I'll tell him to come tomorrow."

John Thomas West was slender and blond, unlike his Native American mother who had dark hair and eyes. Liam hadn't met Maddy's husband Everett but suspected his genes had won. JT was soft-spoken, bordering on shy until Liam showed him how to use the film holders and tilt the 4" x 5" frame to allow for shots that a 35 mm couldn't make. He began asking questions. Smart questions. They eventually took the camera and tripod outside so JT could use the planes of focus on an outdoor subject. He caught on quickly, carefully adjusting the back, tightening the knobs. Fascinated by the possibilities.

Two hours later, Maddy broke up the lesson.

"Sorry Liam, I didn't mean for him to take this much of your time." She turned to JT, "Son, your sister is still waiting for you to pick her up at soccer practice."

JT extended his hand. "Thanks, Mr. Kincaid." Before his mother could say anything else, "I'm leaving, I'm leaving."

"He's a quick study."

"He's been bugging me about this ever since he saw the show the first time."

"I'll take a look online. There might be used cameras out there if he's really interested. The cameras aren't the expensive part, the lenses are. The best ones are German."

"Thanks."

"Have you heard from Kara?"

"She's flying back Thursday." Maddy was a little surprised Liam didn't know that.

Emptying the equipment from the developing lab and studio took longer than Liam anticipated. Once everything was piled on the cabin's living room floor, he began dismantling the stands and lights. Ideally, all the bits and pieces should fit in the SUV so he only had to make one trip to Pecos. Surveying the mess, however, he wasn't sure one trip was going to do it.

In his past life, whenever a major photo project ended, there was always a brief letdown. Working hard and fast—then not working. In those days, other jobs were waiting in the wings, so the sense of anticlimax hung around for only a day or two. This time nothing was waiting.

Definitely his fault.

When he bought the New Mexico land, he'd craved being alone. The isolation was soothing. As he was scrubbing trays, the silence of this cabin was more depressing than soothing. Eventually, he and Sadie took a long walk, getting back just before midnight. She drank all the water in her bowl and crawled into her bed in Liam's room, snoring softly. Liam didn't go to sleep as easily, his mind churning over everything and nothing. When he did drop off, he dreamed about Kara.

And woke up in amazement. For all these years, his dreams had been of Ariane. When had Kara taken up residence is his psyche?

Someone once told him that, when people were learning a second language, they could tell when proficiency with the new language had arrived because their dreams would be in the new language. Did that principle extend to women?

That notion pushed all the guilt buttons and kept him awake the rest of the night.

The day before Liam planned to leave Flagstaff, he received a call from the Dean of the Visual Arts Department at the community college. "I've seen your Colorado Plateau exhibit at the Museum, and I have a proposal I'd like to run by you—if you have time. Maybe tomorrow morning?"

After the call ended, Liam went online to look at Coconino's course catalog. The meeting with Dean Anderson undoubtedly involved speaking to a photography class. He'd occasionally done that in New York.

But the Dean had a different proposal. Just when it seemed no new project was waiting, one fell into Liam's lap.

He needed to touch base with Edgar ASAP.

"Are you free for lunch today?"

"Anything that keeps me from having to eat the nutritious lunch— some of which involves hummus—that my wife packed for me this morning would be appreciated. That means yes."

"If you really want to clog up your arteries, let's do Burger Hut."

"One o'clock?"

"See you then."

Liam arrived five minutes late, put in his order and joined Edgar, who was already seated, a double-decker hamburger and large bag of fries on the table in front of him.

"Sorry. Sadie can be impossibly slow when she knows I want her to hurry with her business."

"I know that routine. What's up? I thought you'd be halfway to New Mexico by now."

"The Dean of the Visual Arts Department at Coconino has offered me a part-time teaching job. He's expanding the photography offerings at the college. Right now, they only do digital photography, but he's adding introductory courses on using and developing black and white film. Old-fashioned photography. NAU doesn't have anything like that so the courses won't be in competition. The C & I committee has already approved everything, and two classes are in the spring schedule. Evening classes for the first go-round. The Spring semester starts the end of January."

Edgar took a bite of the hamburger, wiping his chin. "Damn, that's good. Sue would kill me if she walked in right now."

"I spent an afternoon giving Maddy's son a cram course on using the flat bed camera. It was kind of fun."

"Has Anderson looked at the show?"

"That's what triggered his interest. My problem is housing. Do you think the Museum would go for my renting the cabin for the semester?"

Around another bite, "I don't see why not. It was willed to us about ten years ago, and we haven't used it all that often. You've been the only one this year. I'll run it by Chet. Will you be happy with teaching instead of being out in the field?"

"For the time being, yes. Work that someone else has to arrange and manage looks better than trying to restart a freelance operation. I did that for almost twenty years. It's tough out there. If the classes don't go, I'll have to figure out something else. But I'd like to give it a try."

Liam's order number was called and he hurried to the counter to pick up the tray.

Kara's flight to Phoenix left Honolulu two hours late because there were dangerous winds at Sun Harbor. The delay meant she would arrive around six o'clock, retrieve her car and make the hour plus drive home. She'd originally chosen her flight so she would be home before dark.

Chapter 22

When Jeff left town, Kara asked Maddy if she'd mind being the person notified in case Kara had an emergency. The Museum ID required that it be someone local, and Kara didn't know anyone else. Neither of them thought about it again until Maddy's cell phone rang just before 9 o'clock Thursday evening.

A husky male voice, "Maddy West?"

"Yes. Who is this?"

"Officer Melvin Smith. I'm with the Arizona Highway Patrol."

Since JT was safely watching Thursday Night football with his father, this wasn't about him. She relaxed a little.

"You're listed on Kara Talmadge's ID as the person to be notified in an emergency."

The relaxation disappeared. "Yes I am; what's wrong?"

"We have a major pile-up on Highway 17, involving seven vehicles, one of which belongs to Ms. Talmadge. A semi tractor and trailer jackknifed and set up a chain reaction."

"How is she, where is she?" Maddy was walking into the living room, motioning for her husband to turn the TV sound off. Everett complied.

"She's being transported to the Medical Center in Flagstaff. Sorry, that's all I know at the moment." He ended the call.

Everett was standing beside her. "Who?"

"Kara. There's been a major accident on 17 and they're bringing her here. She was supposed to fly into Phoenix late this afternoon. Her flight must have been delayed. Can you come with me? JT, get yourself and your sister to bed by eleven. There's school tomorrow."

As soon as she got in Everett's truck, she called Liam.

He'd spent the afternoon working on the course outlines the college required for every class. Since these photography classes had never been offered before, he was building them from scratch. He'd spent hours researching what a couple of the major fine arts schools were currently using as textbooks, then ordered two on spec from Amazon so he could check them out. He was struggling with how technical to be. He'd forgotten much of the underlying chemistry and no longer had his old textbooks to refer to. They'd been among the things Tracy disposed of.

Clearly, teaching photography was going to be more complex than doing it. Nevertheless, he was looking forward to the challenge of breaking the process down to the basic level. He had lists and lists of lists lying on the kitchen table.

He was surprised when Maddy's name came up on his cell screen. "Hi, Maddy, what can—"

She interrupted.

He listened. "I'm on my way." When he hit the red button, his hand was shaking. His ragged breathing signaled approaching panic.

Instantly, it was eight years ago. Only this time it was Kara. He felt his chest tighten. *You don't have time for a panic attack.* He forced himself to breathe slowly, deliberately. In—and—out. Until his chest loosened.

He put Sadie on her leash and prayed she wouldn't dawdle.

It was only a ten-minute drive to the Center. The parking lot was full, so he had to wait for a car to pull out. As he was hurrying toward the ER entrance, he punched Maddy's number. When she answered, "I'm just walking inside; are you here or still driving?"

"Just coming into the parking lot, which is jammed. Wait for me. The receptionists probably won't give you any information since you aren't next of kin. At least my name is on her ID."

As he entered the Emergency Room, the organized chaos, the cacophony that surrounds times of human distress washed over him. Triggering the past.

After the NYPD officer standing at his front door delivered the standard *I regret to inform you* message, Liam had been driven to the morgue to identify Ariane's body. He had been in no shape to get himself there. He'd spent years burying the moment the body bag was unzipped and he'd identified Ariane's body. A picture like that is almost impossible to erase. The same officer had been kind enough to drive him home. "Is there someone I can call to come stay with you?"

Liam shook his head. He knew dozens of people, but those people were not who he needed now. He called Tracy, though he wasn't entirely sure he wanted to see her. He needed Ariane. They had been each other's support. No one else mattered.

In the days that followed, others would offer him platitudes because they didn't know what to say. He'd already heard *I'm sorry for your loss* too many times. *Loss* made it sound like he'd carelessly misplaced her somewhere. *Loss* was sidestepping the truth. Call it what it was. The one person who mattered was on a slab inside a refrigerated wall. *Dead.* And from that point on, he was the one who was lost.

He opened a bottle of scotch. It was empty by the time Tracy showed up.

"Liam?" Maddy was standing in front of him, wearing a blue wool coat, a white scarf tied over her hair. "Are you okay?"

He pulled himself back to the present, "Sorry?"

"Are you okay?"

"Not really." *I'm terrified.*

"Let's get some answers." Maddy strode toward the reception counter.

The answers came a little at a time over the next few hours and only slightly reduced the stress that had taken up residence in Liam. The receptionist who took Maddy's name said that there were nine people who

MAKING ROOM

had been injured in the accident, so it could be a while before someone briefed them about Kara.

When Liam started to push for more, Maddy put a hand on his arm. "If she were critical, they'd have her at the front of the line. Let's find a couple of seats, and I'll go look for coffee."

Liam did as he was told, but not happily. He needed to see that Kara was alive, was going to survive. Maddy returned with what passed for coffee from one of the vending machines in the hall. When he tried to repay her, she simply waved him away.

"What happened to Everett?"

"He dropped me off. I'll call him when I'm ready to go home. It's better that he's there so the kids don't stay up all night."

Liam sipped at the bitter coffee. It was comforting to have something to hold onto, but that was about all it was good for. "I've never heard you say what your husband does."

"He works for the city, on the road crew. Twenty years."

"Does he like it?" That type of work had never been on Liam's radar.

"I'm not sure anyone likes laying hot asphalt and fixing potholes, but he mostly drives the various machines those tasks require. And he does like to drive. Which is why JT has a truck already. Not sure JT has the same love of driving, but having his own wheels certainly makes him popular with his friends."

An hour came and went. Patients in the waiting room disappeared into the back halls. New patients took their place. The noise level was constant.

"Should you maybe ask again for information?"

"Nagging usually doesn't help in these kinds of situations. Let's give it some more time."

How could she be so calm? "I'm going outside for a bit. I need air. If you can't save my seat, that's okay." He fled into the freezing night, gulping the fresh air and once again worked on slowing his breathing. On top of his worry about Kara's physical condition, he kept rehearsing what he needed, wanted, to say to her about his retreat over the last weeks. He must apologize for being a coward, for not assuring her that he cared for her. Maybe not in the same way he had loved Ariane. But he wasn't the same man he'd been when he met Ariane. That fact didn't diminish the love. Just made it different; he was different.

Instead, he'd allowed his fear of loving again make him shut her out. And now here he was, like Job: *The thing I greatly feared has come upon me.* He might lose her too.

161

"Liam!" Maddy's voice cut through his thoughts.

He jogged the short distance to the sliding door.

"The doctor is ready for us."

He followed Maddy into a room lined with beds circled with privacy curtains. . "This is Dr. Ruiz."

The young doctor looked exhausted, dark circles around his eyes. He'd obviously had a long shift. He shook their hands. "Sorry for the long wait. We got hit with a lot all at once, and we have several staff members out sick."

"How is she?"

"We've done all the tests we think necessary, including an MRI, that's part of why it's taken so long. She's not awake yet. She has a slight concussion and cracked ribs on both sides, probably from the airbag. No broken bones, but extensive bruising."

"Will she wake up soon?" This from Maddy.

"She should. We're going to let that happen on its own. We've moved her to ICU until she awakens."

"But she'll be okay?" The most important issue for Liam.

"We need to have her awake before we can be sure that there are no other problems."

"May we see her?"

"Are either of you next of kin?"

Maddy shook her head, "But I'm the person who was notified."

"Sorry. The ICU rules are firm. Why don't you leave your phone number with the front desk. We'll notify you when she's awake and has been moved to another room."

Nothing to be done for the moment, so Liam drove Maddy home. He stopped by the cabin to walk Sadie and put on a gray hoodie to hide his hair, slipped on his heaviest coat, then went back to the Medical Center. As though he knew where he was going and was allowed to go there, he bypassed the reception counter and followed the signs to the ICU. Two long, mostly empty halls later, he entered the waiting room next to the Intensive Care nurses' station. He chose a chair in the row farthest from the station, picked up a magazine, put on his reading glasses, and hunched down, hoping that he looked different enough that anyone who'd been in the ER wouldn't recognize him.

He didn't want Kara to wake up in a hospital room, attached to whatever they'd attached her to, without seeing someone she knew. Even though she might not be happy to see him. She hadn't contacted him since she left for Hawaii. But then he hadn't contacted her either. He was the one that had panicked. The ball was definitely in his court.

Whether she would forgive him or not, he intended to be with her when she came around.

Every half hour, one of the nurses went in to check on her. The station had only two nurses for the five units with patients. A little after three o'clock, the older of the two nurses went on a break and, ten minutes later, the emergency alert went off in the unit next to Kara's.

As soon as the nurse left the station, Liam casually walked into Kara's cubicle and pulled the curtains. At some point, he would be asked to leave and not come back, but in the meantime he could at least sit with her.

Pale beneath a tan that she hadn't had when she left Flagstaff, Kara was hooked up to a bag with clear liquid, probably to keep her hydrated. A heart monitor beeped. She looked like she was sleeping peacefully. Her forehead was, however, beginning to show an ugly bruise.

He pulled a straight-backed chair alongside the bed and covered her hand, careful not to move it. Sitting here was trespassing on her vulnerability. Regardless, he needed to see that she was breathing, that her heart was pumping. That she was alive. He needed to have her alive.

Love announced itself in subtle ways.

Until this moment, that need hadn't really settled into his thinking, into his emotions. He'd probably rushed sleeping with her. He'd gotten ahead of himself after Dr. Elaine's lecture about not wasting his life. Letting Kara think he was ready for more when he probably hadn't been. But the moment Maddy called, the moment he confronted the possibility of losing her, he knew he needed her to be safe—needed her.

"Who told you that you could be here?" The voice was impatient.

Pushing the hoodie back, he stood to face the voice. "No one. I just didn't want her to be alone when she woke up." The nurse was younger than the harsh tone suggested. Thin face, pale blonde hair pulled back.

"Please leave."

A soft whisper interrupted. "I'd like him to stay."

Kara's voice.

The nurse moved to the bed. "Mrs. Talmadge. Are you in any pain?"

"Sore. Hard to breathe."

"That's because you have cracked ribs." The nurse looked into Kara's eyes, took her pulse. "Do you know what day it is?"

"I came home Thursday. The plane was late. Then cars all over the road. So is it Friday now?"

The nurse nodded, "Do you know who this man is?"

Kara's voice was slightly stronger. "Liam. We work together."

A phone rang somewhere beyond the room. "I need to answer that." To Liam, "You can stay a few minutes."

He sat down and reached for Kara's hand again. "They said you'll be okay." Well they hadn't really said it that way, but he wanted her to feel confident.

"How did you get in here?"

"I have a devious streak. I waited until no one was watching. She'll send for the doctor because you're awake and I'll get tossed."

"Thanks for coming."

"You scared me."

"I scared me. I think my car is totaled."

"That's solvable."

This time the nurse had a doctor with her. "Now you have to leave."

Liam raised Kara's hand and kissed her palm.

He returned to the chair he'd been occupying in the waiting room and called Maddy. Even though it was the middle of the night, she would want to know Kara was awake.

"Liam? What time is it?"

"In the neighborhood of three o'clock. She's awake. And cogent. Worried about her car."

"Did they let you talk to her?"

He grinned, "*Let* is not quite the correct word. I have, quite firmly, been banished."

He heard Maddy laughing as she ended the call.

Chapter 23

Kara slept through being moved to another room, only waking when breakfast arrived at six a.m.. An impossibly early hour. She was groggy, unsure whether the images wandering around in her head were real or not. A montage of the accident—cars akimbo on the road in front of her—too close—and then being smacked by the airbag. Somewhere in the montage, she remembered Liam being in her hospital room.

She was sore all over and desperate to brush her teeth. Other than the orange juice, breakfast did not look appetizing. Yogurt and, by now, cold barely buttered toast.

She tried to be grateful she was alive and not permanently damaged—arms and legs moved, her mid-section moved painfully. Gratitude was all well and good, but right now it was doing battle with self-pity. She'd survived Michael's death, then Jeff's departure, Lindsay and Malia moving to the other side of the globe. When did she get a say in what happened to her? Why hadn't she wanted a say years earlier? And after all the back and forth with Liam this last year, she wasn't entirely certain that a man, any man, was the answer to improving her life.

This was, however, probably not the morning to reevaluate her circumstances.

So she went back to sleep.

At the cabin, Liam took a shower, walked Sadie, then called Kara's children, using the phone numbers Maddy had provided last night. They needed to know about the accident. When he finished talking to Lindsay, Maddy called.

"I understand they've moved her."

"I'm glad you checked. After tossing me out of the ICU last night, they might not take my call."

"She's in a double room, 358. I'm working this morning. Can you check in on her later?"

"I intend to. Just need to clean up and take care of Sadie."

"Let me know how she is."

Instead of looking for a florist, Liam stopped at the Safeway to pick up a bouquet of mixed flowers that came with a vase, checked in at the nurses' station on the third floor, and was told the doctor was with Kara. Liam could go in as soon as the doctor finished. "Wait over there." The nurse pointed to chairs lining a wall.

A few minutes later, Liam intercepted the doctor in the hall. "How is she?"

The doctor hesitated, "Weren't you in the ICU last night? What's your relationship to Ms. Talmadge?"

"I'm Liam Kincaid. We work together. She doesn't have any relatives close by."

Thankfully, the doctor decided to trust him. "Her vitals are good. She's much improved. Since she lives alone however, we're keeping her for another day or two. I want to make sure about the concussion."

Cautioning Liam against staying too long, he walked to the nurses' station.

Liam paused in Kara's doorway, a rush of relief hitting him. She was no longer hooked up to machines, but she still looked fragile. The bruise on her forehead a whirl of red and orange.

"Good morning. I'm not supposed to stay long."

Kara smiled at the sight of the flowers. "Pretty. Is someone sick?"

He tried to match her tone. "Fortunately, no." His throat tightened dangerously. "I like your new makeup."

"I haven't looked at myself, but it's really sore, actually everything's sore."

He placed the vase on a small table next to the window on her side of the room and sat beside the bed.

She was alive.

She would get better.

He kept running that loop through his head.

"What do you need?"

"A better breakfast." She stopped, carefully taking a breath. "Someone retrieved my purse. My phone was hooked up to the car," another careful breath, "guess it's gone. My suitcase too." The effort of just that much talking made her ribs scream.

"I'll find out about your car. Maddy said it was towed."

"Can you call Maddy for me?"

"Already did, Jeff and Lindsay as well."

"Oh." She closed her eyes for a moment.

"I can get whatever you want from your place."

She forced her eyes open, "Maybe Maddy can bring me some clothes— and shampoo."

Before she could spell out what else she wanted, she was asleep again.

After ten minutes, Liam left the Center, stopping at the Museum to see Maddy. She promised to get clothes and toiletries from Kara's during her lunch break.

Liam looked up the address for the Highway Patrol office to see about Kara's car. The insurance information should be in the glove compartment, so long as the glove compartment was still in one piece. If he was lucky, her cell phone might have survived the crash.

By mid-afternoon, Liam had dealt with some of the business surrounding the accident. Kara's car had been towed to a wrecking yard west of town. Once again, not being related to her was a barrier. He couldn't pick up her suitcase or the contents of the glove compartment until Kara signed a permission form. Her cell phone was gone, so he bought a pre-paid one at Wal-Mart. She'd want to talk to her kids. He programmed their numbers in, as well as his own and Maddy's.

It was nearly five o'clock when he made it back to the cabin. Sadie was not amused. "Sorry girl. Today, Kara comes first." He was fairly sure the hospital did not allow dogs, but a visit from Sadie might be just what Kara needed.

Before heading to the hospital, he tried Maddy's cell.

"Did you have time to take her clothes over or should I stop by your place?"

"I'm with her now."

"And?"

"They say she's improving by the minute; she agrees, except for being sore. They've decided the concussion isn't a threat, but they don't want her to be at home by herself. So they're sending her to rehab for a few days."

In the background, he could hear Kara's voice.

"She says to bring a sandwich."

He laughed. "Done."

A nurse was clearing away the remains of dinner when Liam entered Kara's room. Seeing what was on the tray, he understood her sandwich request.

Tonight, she looked more like Kara. Her eyes were clear, her hair was combed and she'd changed into one of her own nightgowns. As soon as the nurse was gone, he leaned to kiss her cheek. "You look better. And you're awake."

"I've slept most of the day. I'll probably be awake all night." She reached for the sack. "My sandwich?"

"BLT. Almost got pastrami but I figured the smell would give the contraband away."

She opened the sack and pulled out half of the sandwich. "I'm starving. The size and quality of the meals here leave a lot to be desired." Around her chewing, "Oh, totally delicious. Thank you."

He sat down, enjoying her enjoying the sandwich. One of those comfortable silences they had always been good at. Simple pleasures.

She'd missed him, missed his eyes narrowing when he smiled, like he was smiling now. Remembered all the other parts of him currently covered by clothing. Too bad he was here only because she'd been injured.

As she finished the sandwich, he handed her another sack. She looked inside, "Fries! You're up for sainthood."

"Catsup packets on top."

"I'll save these for later. I'm full. Thank you."

"Your appetite has certainly returned. How do you feel?"

"Stiff and sore. My brain seems to be working better, and the doctor says he's willing to sign me out tomorrow. He's talking about putting me in rehab for a few days so I won't be home alone. Probably wise. Moving around and walking up stairs might not be easy."

He reached for her hand. "I could come stay with you if you want to be at home."

She thought about it—probably too long. "I think rehab will be better."

All of a sudden he was moving too fast for her current state of mind. The very thing she had been wanting just might be available, but now she wasn't quite ready to make that leap. He kept taking two steps forward, then one back. She wasn't going to get her hopes up only to have him retreat again and again and again.

Sleep was tugging at her.

Trying to hide his disappointment about her rehab decision, "I located your car. Your suitcase and everything in the glove compartment are at the wrecking yard." He laid the prepaid phone on the table. "The phone didn't make it. Or someone pinched it. Use this one until you can get a better one." He handed her his pen and the form, "And you have to sign this so I can abscond with your suitcase. Everything by the book. It does slow down solving problems."

Kara signed carefully. "Thank you."

The family of the woman in the other bed had arrived around eight o'clock, raising the noise level in the room.

"Maybe I should go. Your eyes are trying to go to sleep again."

"Can't seem to keep that from happening."

"Before I go, I want to show you something."

He turned on his iPhone and opened the photo app, scrolling. "Here."

Kara looked at it, frowning. "It's a blank wall."

"In my living room—in Pecos."

She looked again. "Where are the photos?"

"I took them down."

Caught off guard, she didn't say anything.

"I put them in storage. Edgar's making arrangements with the Museum for me to enlarge several of the photos from the show."

He stopped before he pushed too hard, too soon. *Too soon* had already failed.

Kara still didn't know what to say. Just when she thought he could never leave his past behind, he made a major change.

"I wanted you to know." He paused, "You're tired." He kissed her lips this time, "I'll be back tomorrow."

Her eyes were closed when the nurse checked on her, but Kara wasn't asleep.

Chapter 24

K ara spent Christmas day alone.

She was too worn out to celebrate, though she did skype with both children on Christmas Eve. Lindsay was expecting Max the day after Christmas. The baby was fine; Lindsay was fine. The surf was *Awesome*. Clearly her daughter was back to normal. Kara almost asked who was taking care of Malia while Lindsay was surfing but chose not to ruin their conversation.

She turned down Maddy's Christmas dinner invitation—she wasn't up to that much socializing—but gratefully accepted the heaping plate of ham and sides that JT delivered. She enjoyed the mini-feast while watching a BBC special featuring the Vienna Boys Choir and turned in early. Being alone on the holiday was oddly pleasant. Since leaving rehab, she'd kept Liam at arm's length. This time she was the one backing away. Rumor had it that he spent Christmas at Edgar's. At her request, he didn't call.

Fortunately, Kara had shopped for Jeff's children when she was in Cincinnati and wisely left the packages there. Malia was too young to know whether or not Nana had bought her a gift. Kara made a list of the Christmas cards she received. She'd have to find *mea culpa* cards to send later so no one would think she'd died.

She could have died.

That fact insisted on crawling, uninvited, into her consciousness. What if she had? What would she regret, what should she have done that she had not done? She'd never liked the idea of a Bucket List, but she'd never come so close to dying. Were there things Michael wished he'd done? Ariane too.

As the soreness eased and she could move more easily, she felt less and less sure about the future. Rather like the year after Michael's death. Here without being here.

Her art class was the only event on her horizon. Ten children were registered, with a short waiting list. While she was recovering, she'd sent the art store a list of the supplies each child should have. A medium-sized pad of Watercolor paper, a beginner's pan of watercolors, a few brushes—at least one that was two-inches wide. A small sketchbook, three HB pencils for drawing and practicing shading. She designed a series of handouts with shapes for them to use as subjects: Apples, a backpack, an Iris, a car. It was a start.

She would be creating the course content as she went along because each child would require something different. She was actually looking forward to figuring everything out. She could feel her passion for painting reemerging.

Her passion for Liam was on hold.

The first week of January, the doctor gave Kara her walking papers. "I don't need to see you until the end of the month, just to make sure the ribs are stable." The Subaru agency had found a three-year old blue sedan with 30,000 miles to replace her Outback. In theory, everything was back to normal. But she was looking for a new normal. She needed to stop letting others interfere with her life. To stop assuming she had to accommodate others' needs instead of her own. She was no longer automatically available for diaper changing or dog sitting, though she did miss Sadie.

She'd gotten the post-Michael phase of her life backward. Figuring herself out should have been the first thing she did after he died. For the first time, it occurred to her that she'd never—*never* made herself a priority. As a college student, besotted with Michael and unexpectedly pregnant, she willingly gave up her art and college to be a wife and mother. That's what young women were supposed to do. And then, like a human tumbleweed, she let life push her here and there. The most astonishing part: she'd been content.

Before she could consider any kind of life with Liam, if he wanted one with her, she had to know what she could do, who she could be—with or without him. She was standing on a precipice

The day Liam drove her home from rehab, she had explained the precipice.

And he took her request for space seriously. Listened without commenting. She explained that, like his putting off grief therapy, she'd put off adjusting to being on her own, to calling her own shots. She'd made some mistakes while she was married, followed more than walked alongside Michael and the children. She wasn't sure she knew how to walk beside, let alone in front.

Liam was careful not to touch her—no kissing, no handholding. No hints that they had briefly been more than friends. Kara wanted space; he could give her space. She'd certainly done the same for him. Maybe they would never be on the same page at the same time. Maybe they'd missed or never had the chance of being more.

The first two weeks of the art class flew by. Seven girls and three boys, the youngest five, the oldest ten. A perfect group to practice on. One of the boys, Peter, was a natural. His mother said he was drawing on everything as soon as he could hold a crayon. He was so far ahead of the others that Kara was preparing more difficult subjects for him to work on.

Encouraged by how much pleasure the art classes were giving her, she hired JT and one of his friends to take apart the bed in the guest room, storing the mattress and bed frame in the garage. She bought a basic art table and lamp, found a stool that looked moderately comfortable, and had everything delivered to what was turning into her studio. Goodbye guest room. She needed to unpack her paintings and the few supplies she'd kept all these years. None of the paint would be any good; maybe some of the brushes had survived if she'd cleaned them well before packing them away.

Putting the studio together and sorting through her old paintings was fun. She set them on the floor, leaning them against the walls throughout the house so she could study what she had done well. And what she'd failed at. She'd worked in both oil and watercolor. Oil might be easier to start with. In that case, she'd need an easel of some kind. She started a list.

When The Art Depot advertised a sale on canvas, Kara invested in several different sizes, even one that had a deep cradle. She'd never used one of those. Maybe they hadn't been available thirty years ago. She primed them, then set up a 14" x 18" canvas on her new tabletop easel, chose a half-finished seascape and began copying it. Baby steps. She needed to remember what the paint felt like, how it moved on the surface. Halfway through the painting, she set that canvas aside and started over. She needed the practice.

When she was happy with the seascape, she started a still life. At the beginning of March, Ellen had emailed several photos of the children so, for her third project, Kara was considering capturing them on canvas.

Two weeks into Kara's second group of classes, Edgar sent her a text: **Liam would like you to look at the page proofs on the Plateau photo book. We signed off on them two days ago. Since it's Spring Break, he's in Pecos seeing about the broken pump on his well. Let me know when you can come in.**

Kara suggested Friday afternoon.

I have to be in Williams on Friday. I'll leave them on the table in my office.

She hadn't been at the Museum since she left for Hawaii. When she entered the lobby, Maddy had several people waiting so Kara went straight to Edgar's empty office. As promised, the stack of page proofs was on the table. She rolled his desk chair over and carefully turned to the title page:

Colorado Plateau Artisans
Liam Kincaid, Photographer
The next page was filled with copyright/publishing data
On the third page:
Dedicated to Kara, who cares about this project as much as I do
The page blurred.

It was a while before she moved on to another page. The tribute touched her heart, but she was afraid to read too much into it. Halfway through the pages, she turned back to the beginning. This time she needed to pay attention to the photographs instead of thinking about Liam. About having the book dedicated to her.

Spring was trying to come to Pecos—green shoots here and there. Cool nights and warm days. Liam had missed the way the scent of pines mingled with the pungent dryness of the soil. This beautiful, peaceful place always relaxed him. The pump problem was solved more easily than he expected, so he and Johnny played tennis one morning, ending up at the diner for lunch.

"Could you help me hang some large photos at the cabin?"

"You took the French collection down?"

"A few months ago."

"So what are the replacements?"

"Duplicates of four of the Plateau portraits."

"Sorry I didn't get over to see the show at the Museum."

"No problem. The Museum is putting them out as a coffee table book. I'll make sure you get a copy."

The waitress brought two beers and took their orders.

They spent most of the meal catching up with Johnny's life, Sadie, and Liam's experiment with teaching. "Sometimes I leave a class thinking I've totally failed and, other times, I'm amazed at how well the evening has gone. So far, no middle ground."

"How's Kara?"

"Okay, I guess. She's on her second round of children's art classes. And she's started painting again. To advertise the classes, the art store has a seascape of hers displayed in the window," Liam paused, "it's really good."

"But you haven't seen her?"

Liam shook his head. "Her request."

Johnny signaled for another beer. "You okay with that?"

Liam shrugged.

"I'm guessing my prying into your love life is not welcome."

"Correct. Can you help hang the new photos tomorrow?"

The day an elderly couple, originally from Santa Barbara, walked into the art store and bought the seascape painting—*it reminds us of home*—Kara felt as though she were walking on air. Edith asked if she had another painting to replace it.

"A still life I just finished." She and Edith split the seascape's sale price 50/50. It wasn't the money that made Kara's heart race; it was the validation of the path she was choosing.

Her excitement needed to be shared.

After a quick dinner of scrambled eggs and toast, she drove to the Museum cabin. Liam's car was in the narrow driveway but neither he nor Sadie was there. Undoubtedly on a walk. She sat on the top step and waited, not entirely sure what she was going to say. She simply needed to share her news. And Liam was the person she most wanted to share it with.

Forty-five minutes later, she saw them walking toward the cabin. Sadie wasn't moving very fast, so they must have gone a long way. In the darkness, Liam didn't see Kara until he was almost at the porch and Sadie was tugging at her leash. He undid it so she could get to Kara.

"Hi. Have you been waiting long?"

"A while. Long walk?"

"Sadie's been cooped up a lot lately, what with the rain and snow and my schedule, so I thought we both needed the exercise. She gave up about ten minutes ago and lay down for a rest. She's too heavy to carry so I let her decide when we'd continue." He sat down beside Kara while Sadie received her petting.

He waited for Kara to say something.

And waited.

He couldn't handle the silence. "It's nice to see you." Not what he really wanted to say.

Her words tumbled out. "I just wanted to tell you that I sold a painting, the seascape in the window at the art store." Every inch of her face was smiling.

"Congratulations. Someone local?"

"Yes. They're originally from Santa Barbara and they miss the ocean."

"It's a beautiful painting."

"You saw it?"

"Several times."

"Really?"

"I've missed you. It made me feel better to look at your painting."

"I had to do it twice."

"Is that a problem? I've certainly had to retake photos."

"I'm having to relearn a lot. I'm replacing it with another one I just finished. It's a still life of old-fashioned baby dolls and teddy bears. I originally started it when I was pregnant with Jeff but was never happy with the results." She was fairly sure she was talking too much.

"I'm glad you're painting." Her joy was contagious.

"I am too. Edgar said you were in Pecos."

"The electric pump on the well quit working. It was old."

"Was it good to be home?"

"Yes and no." He'd felt Kara's absence more than he could have imagined. She'd only been at his cabin twice, yet he could see her everywhere. The house was too quiet. He wanted her with him.

The conversation ran aground. Smoothing Sadie's fur gave Kara something to focus on.

Maybe she'd permanently ruined everything by asking for space. She needed to tell him so many things. To thank him for giving her time, to apologize for needing time.

To fill the silence, Liam tried out the question he'd been rehearsing in his head.

"Would you go out on a date with me? Just a date, for dinner or a movie or both. No assumptions."

Very softly. "I'd like that."

"One date at a time. Starting over."

She could hardly believe what she was hearing. "It sounds—perfect."

Sadie padded to the front door.

Liam stood up. "She's thirsty. Will you come inside for a while?"

"I'd like that."

A major understatement.

Acknowledgement

Many thanks to my friend Joal for "loaning" me Sadie.

Printed in the United States
By Bookmasters